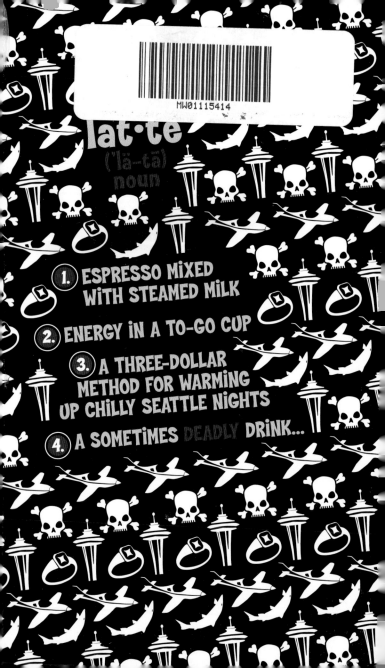

MW01115414

lat·te
('lä-tä)
noun

1. ESPRESSO MiXED WiTH STEAMED MiLK

2. ENERGY iN A TO-GO CUP

3. A THREE-DOLLAR METHOD FOR WARMiNG UP CHiLLY SEATTLE NiGHTS

4. A SOMETiMES DEADLY DRiNK...

CRASH

Seth grabbed my hand and pulled me back by him and my mom.

"Tie yourself in!" she yelled.

We wrapped the nets and the ties and anything else we could find around us as the plane bucked one last time. The propellers sputtered. The sound of the engines died. My stomach tumbled as the g-force pressed me back against the wall.

"Put your head between your knees!" Mom yelled. "Lock your hands behind your head like this!" She illustrated, lacing her fingers.

I followed her directions, trying to stay as calm as she appeared to be, but my hands shook and tears welled in my eyes.

"We're going to be okay," she yelled.

I nodded, even though I wasn't so sure.

She broke her crash position and gave me a rough hug. "I love you, Aphra," she said hoarsely. "No matter what happens, always remember that." I hugged her back—for the first time in four years—just before we went down.

OTHER SLEUTH BOOKS YOU MAY ENJOY

LINDA GERBER'S *DEATH BY* SERIES

Death by Bikini

Death by Latte

Death by Denim

DEATH BY Latte

LINDA GERBER

SLEUTH
SPEAK
An Imprint of Penguin Group (USA) Inc.

For my girls

SLEUTH / SPEAK
Published by the Penguin Group
Penguin Group (USA) Inc., 345 Hudson Street, New York, New York 10014, U.S.A.
Penguin Group (Canada), 90 Eglinton Avenue East, Suite 700,
Toronto, Ontario, Canada M4P 2Y3 (a division of Pearson Penguin Canada Inc.)
Penguin Books Ltd, 80 Strand, London WC2R 0RL, England
Penguin Ireland, 25 St Stephen's Green, Dublin 2, Ireland (a division of Penguin Books Ltd)
Penguin Group (Australia), 250 Camberwell Road, Camberwell, Victoria 3124, Australia
(a division of Pearson Australia Group Pty Ltd)
Penguin Books India Pvt Ltd, 11 Community Centre,
Panchsheel Park, New Delhi - 110 017, India
Penguin Group (NZ), 67 Apollo Drive, Rosedale, North Shore 0632, New Zealand
(a division of Pearson New Zealand Ltd.)
Penguin Books (South Africa) (Pty) Ltd, 24 Sturdee Avenue,
Rosebank, Johannesburg 2196, South Africa

Registered Offices: Penguin Books Ltd, 80 Strand, London WC2R 0RL, England

This Sleuth edition published by Speak,
an imprint of Penguin Group (USA) Inc., 2008

5 7 9 10 8 6 4

Copyright © Linda Gerber, 2008
All rights reserved

CIP Data is available.

Speak ISBN 978-0-14-241118-6

Printed in the United States of America

Acknowledgments

They say that being a writer is a solitary pursuit, but that just isn't so. The making of a book takes much more than just the efforts of the author; it takes an entire team of smart people working together. It has been my good fortune to work with the best of the best.

As always, special thanks to my family for their encouragement and for picking up the slack when I wander off into the writing zone. GUSH to my CPs: Jen, Ginger, Barb, Nicole, Julie, Kate, Karen, and Marsha.

Resounding thank-you to Diane Lutz, Christine Solberg, and Wendy Clark of the Greater Seattle RWA for sharing their experience and perspective and for having the patience to answer countless questions.

Words cannot adequately express my gratitude to the good folks at Puffin for their continued work and support. Huge, HUGE thanks to the sales team for spreading the love, to designers Theresa Evangelista and Linda McCarthy for giving me the best covers ever, and especially to my phenom editor Angelle Pilkington and to Grace Lee for their collective editorial genius. Working with you all has been a sincere pleasure!

DEATH BY LATTE

CHAPTER 1

lied to my dad. That's how the whole thing started. I told him I was going to South Carolina to visit a friend, but instead I hopped a flight to Seattle. It made complete sense at the time, but being alone and far from home can make a huge difference in perspective. And lies have a strange way of catching up to you in ways you never imagined.

You have to understand my situation: I hadn't seen my mom in four years. She stayed behind when my dad left for the Pacific to open an exclusive island resort. He took me with him . . . and she let me go. She never came to visit. Not once. All I wanted was to see her again. I didn't intend for things to go so terribly wrong.

Looking back, I guess I should have known better; before we even touched down in Seattle, my stomach felt like it had been stuffed with broken glass. I suppose my body was trying to tell me what my head refused to accept—that sneaking off wasn't such a great idea.

By the time the taxi dropped me off in front of Pike Place Market, I was having serious second thoughts . . . but it was a little late for that then. All I could do was wait for the Market to open, find my mom, and hope she'd be happy to see me.

Oh, yeah. Did I mention that I hadn't told her I was coming?

That part is not my fault. I might have told her if I'd had the option, but I didn't have any way of contacting her. The only reason I even knew where to find her was that a mutual friend had let me in on the secret. But that's a whole other story.

My flight got into Seattle at eight that morning. The Market didn't open until ten. So even after the taxi ride, I had over an hour to wait. That hour passed excruciatingly slowly. It probably didn't help that I kept checking the glowing plate-shaped clock over the entrance every two minutes, but I couldn't help it. Now that the wait was almost over, each passing second was torture.

Delivery trucks came and went. Tarp-covered carts clattered over the bricks around me. Vendors called out greetings to one another as they hauled buckets of bright flowers and crates of vegetables and fish inside the arcade. *They* all seemed to move in real time, so why did the minutes tick by in slow motion?

I had to literally force myself to turn away from the clock. Obsessing wasn't going to do me any good. I had to find something—anything—to take my mind off the time or I'd to go crazy. Some of the shops across the street looked like they were open, so I wandered over to take a look.

Shop windows framed everything from fresh pastries to Native American art, but none of the displays really registered. Even the aroma of fresh coffee and frying dough from the coffee shops couldn't draw my attention. Physically I might have been looking in windows, but mentally I was still counting down minutes.

Finally, I noticed people filing through the main entrance. The doors were open. My stomach began to churn again. Now that the moment had arrived, I wasn't sure I was ready for it.

I hugged my arms and trudged back across the street. Just inside the entrance, people clustered four or five deep around a fish stand. They were all gawking at something, but I couldn't tell what. I worked my way through the crowd until I saw a worker in orange-and-black overalls in front of the long glass counter, his finger hooked through the gills of a huge silvery fish. He was talking to a lady in a floral sundress, projecting his voice like a stage actor.

"What time's your flight?" he asked.

"Three."

"Where do you live?"

"San Diego."

"Are you single?"

The crowd laughed and the sundress lady blushed prettily. The fish guy hefted the fish and flung it over his head. "One king salmon packed for California!"

The salmon flew through the air to where another worker behind the counter stood waiting with a sheet of brown paper. The fish slapped into his arms and he wrapped the paper around it in one fluid movement. "One king salmon packed for California!"

The first guy worked the crowd, posing for pictures, hawking the fish, joking with the customers. I watched for a couple of minutes, but I realized I was just avoiding the inevitable.

I eased behind a guy in a Mariners jersey, and as had become habit when I was anxious, my hand reached for the ring that hung on a chain around my neck. It had been only months since Seth Mulo gave me that ring, but it seemed like much longer. A lot had happened since then; my dad had gone in and out of the hospital, the CIA agents looking for Seth's family had invaded every possible sanctuary on the island, we had closed and then reopened the resort, and I had lied to my dad and flown two thousand miles to find my mom. Through it all, I could never shake that tingle-in-the-back sensation that I was being watched.

Just thinking about it made the hairs at the back of my neck prickle. I fought the urge to sneak a glance over my shoulder. With all the other doubts and misgivings in my head, the last thing I needed was to let paranoia crowd in among them. I tucked the ring under my shirt and turned from the fishmongers. I'd worry about the other stuff later. After I found my mom.

Unfortunately, I didn't have the slightest idea where

to begin looking for her. I didn't see a booth directory posted anywhere and the arcade corridor was a confusion of carts and booths and storefronts.

The closest stall belonged to a local jewelry artist, according to the banner that hung above his workspace. The center of the table had been draped in black velvet and held an impressive display of silver bracelets, charms, and chains. An elderly gentleman—the artist, I presume—sat behind the table, bent over the new piece he was crafting.

I approached hesitantly. "Excuse me."

He looked up, woolly eyebrows raised.

"I'm sorry to bother you, but do you know where Pike's Pottery is?"

The man scratched his beard with the silver tool he'd been working with. "Couldn't tell ya. Prob'ly down the hall or outside."

"They don't have a regular spot?"

"Naw. Most of us are whatcha call day-stallers. We get our space location assignments at morning roll call."

With that, he went back to his work. I mumbled my thanks and scanned the crowded arcade once again. I didn't understand exactly how the space thing worked, but I got the part that mattered: Pike's Pottery could be anywhere in the Market. I would have to look for it.

People of all sizes and shapes flowed into the arcade and down the corridor like a swift-rising river and I allowed myself to be swept along with the current, craning my neck to look at the booths as I passed each one.

Heavy perfume from incense and flower carts swirled about my head. Harmonica music drifted through the air. The produce guy across the hall laughed, his voice booming over the noise of the crowd. "Hey, you squeeze it, you buy it!"

Finally, on the other side of the corridor, I spotted a booth practically groaning under the weight of a collection of pots and bowls, vases and urns. A tall, dark-haired guy stood behind the table, absently dusting each piece. No banner advertised the name of the business, but I figured if it wasn't Pike's Pottery, at least the guy might be able to tell me where that booth was, assuming that he kept track of his competitors.

I had almost reached the booth when a woman carrying what looked like a very heavy cardboard box squeezed into the space behind the booth, nudging the man out of her way. My breath caught. Her hair was different from when I'd seen her last—shorter and maybe a little darker. The bohemian skirt and gauzy shirt were worlds away from the khakis and jeans she used to wear, and four years ago, she never would have been caught dead in all the drippy beads and chains hanging around her neck. But the rest of her looked the same. Ordinary. Average. She looked like me.

My feet stopped working. I couldn't move, so I just

stood there and let people bump past me as I stared at my mom. I swallowed against the huge lump that swelled in my throat. This was it. No turning back.

Smoothing my hair with a shaky hand, I forced myself to walk forward. Mom looked up as I approached the booth.

"How can I help . . ." Her words died and she blinked at me. "Aphra?" she whispered.

Everything I had intended to say when I first saw her vanished and all I could come up with was "Hi, Mom." For the briefest of moments, I saw something joyful flicker behind her eyes. It gave me hope. But then, right before my eyes, her face went blank. Truly. It's like she purposefully erased all expression until the only thing left was an empty canvas with no feeling, no warmth.

My heart tumbled right into my stomach. It's not like I'd expected her to go all misty and climb over the table to sweep me into her arms or anything, but it might have been nice if she could have at least pretended to be happy to see me.

Instead she just frowned. "What are you doing here?"

What did she *think* I was doing? "I came to see you."

The tall dark guy stepped up beside her and jerked his chin in my direction. "What's going on? Who's this?"

"This," Mom said, "is my daughter." Her tone was distant. Annoyed. I swallowed my confusion.

His eyes narrowed and he looked me over like I

might spread disease or something. "Your *kid*? She can't be here. Get rid of her."

My mouth hung open. *Get rid of me?* I couldn't believe he was being so blatantly rude. I waited for Mom to chew him out, but she just stood there looking at me with that stupid vacant expression on her face. "Aphra," she said evenly, "you need to leave."

"Leave? I just got here!"

Her eyebrow twitched, but otherwise she gave no indication that she had even heard what I said. "Joe?" Her eyes never left me. "Hand me the keys, would you?"

The guy slapped a set of keys into her hand and she stepped out from behind the stall, gesturing with her head. "Come with me."

I planted my feet and folded my arms. "I'm not going anywhere."

Still, no emotion registered on her face. She slipped her arm around my waist and leaned close, lowering her voice. "Aphra, this really is not the time or place."

"Well, I'm sorry," I whispered back, "but you haven't really given me a lot of other options, have you?"

Her calm expression flickered once again. What was that behind her veiled eyes? Amusement? Exasperation? "Come with me. We can talk outside."

At least that was something. I allowed her to steer me toward the wide portico, and I swear I could feel Joe's glare on my back the entire way.

Sunlight stabbed my eyes the moment we stepped through the door and I drew back, but Mom nudged me forward. I stumbled ahead, squinting in the harsh light. From what I could actually see in those moments before my eyes fully adjusted, the street had filled with the same bright jigsaw puzzle of vendor carts, stalls, and flower booths as inside the arcade. Outside, though, there was the added attraction of street entertainers. On one corner, a violinist offered an intricate, lush melody. On the other, a guy with a couple of spoons beat out the rhythm of the song against his thigh. We had to skirt around a cluster of people watching a man in a Technicolor vest twist long, skinny balloons into unlikely shapes.

Mom walked briskly, like she was late for a business meeting or something. I had to practically run to keep up with her. "Mom, I'm sorry I didn't call you first, but—"

She shot me a quick look and shook her head just enough for me to get the meaning. "Don't speak," she said in a low voice.

Mom didn't, either. Speak, that is. Not until we walked halfway down the street, where the crowd thinned out. "What are you doing here?" she finally asked. "How did you get here?"

The tone of her voice took me back to another time and place. When I was about ten, I had gotten hurt riding my Schwinn down a steep and rocky dirt-bike path that I had been forbidden to try until I was older. Mom tried to be stern with me when she found out what happened, but she couldn't quite hide her concern behind her words. My throat suddenly felt tight and achy. I took several steps before answering. "I flew."

"Aphra, I'm serious. How did you find me?" She glanced over her shoulder before adding, "The Smiths?"

"Ha." When Seth and his family had come to our resort, they had registered under the name of Smith. Since Mom was the one who had sent them to us, she was probably the author of that creative alias, but we both knew their name was Mulo.

"Mrs. Mulo told me where to find you," I whispered.

Mom's lips squashed into a straight line. "She should not have done that." Her pace quickened as she led me down a steep sidewalk to a parking area tucked beneath the raised freeway. We wove between parked cars and concrete support pillars, traffic whooshing overhead. She stopped next to a dirty white Econoline van, and pulled out the keys.

"Where are we going?" I asked.

She didn't even look up, but unlocked the passenger-side door and opened it. "To the airport. You can't stay here."

I took a step back. "No."

Whatever softness or concern I thought I had heard before vanished. "Excuse me?"

"I told you before; I'm not leaving."

"Aphra, you don't understand. I'm not asking—"

"No. *You* don't understand. You owe me, Mom. I've

waited four years to get some answers from you, and I'm not leaving until I do."

Mom signaled me to be quiet while a woman with a stroller passed by, and then she nudged me toward the van. "We're not going to have this conversation here."

I pulled away. I had waited too long to talk to her and spent a good chunk of my resort earnings to buy the plane ticket for the opportunity. There was no way I was going to let her send me home without an explanation. I just wouldn't go. What was she going to do? Carry me onto the *plane*? "We're not going to have the conversation at the airport, either," I said.

She gritted her teeth. "I see. Please get in."

I raised a brow at her forced civility and matched it with my own. "I'd prefer not to."

"We'll go someplace where we can talk."

I folded my arms and stared her down.

"You have my word," she said.

Once, her word might have meant something to me, but she was no longer the mom I used to know. I had no idea if her word was worth a thing anymore, but I really wanted to believe it was. Which is why I caved. I shrugged my backpack from my shoulders, swung it into the van, and then climbed in after it.

Inside, ceramic dust coated the cargo area and clung like microscopic barnacles to the front console and the seats. It smelled old and dry. The closing door behind me sounded like the bars of a prison cell clanging shut. That would have been a good time to cut my losses and go home. But, of course, I wasn't about to do that.

Mom climbed into her side and settled onto the seat, turning the key in the ignition and checking the rearview. Her actions were all very calm and measured, but irritation was clearly written on her face. I folded my arms tight across my chest and I turned my own face to the window so she wouldn't see the angry tears gathering in my eyes.

I suppose I had known all along that my surprise appearance might not go over well. Mom had a life, after all, and I had interrupted it. But what did *she* have to be mad about? She's the one who left all those years ago. If anything, *I* should be the one pulling faces and acting all put out about things.

We drove in silence for what felt like a very long time. Mom didn't say anything, and I wasn't about to talk just to fill the void. I did steal glances at her, though. Her expression never changed.

"What did you want to talk about?" she finally asked.

I stared at her. "Are you kidding?"

She didn't reply.

I turned back to the window. She left the main road for a steep side street where she pulled over to the curb to park.

"Aphra, I'm sorry you're upset, but you can't just show up out of the blue like this. Not now. There are things you don't know . . ."

"But I *do* know." I swung to face her. "I know you were with the CIA. I know you left Dad and me to help protect the Mulos when the agency no longer would. I know you sent their family to stay with us because you thought it was the one place where no one would find them. But that's over now, Mom. They're gone and I'm here. It's my turn now."

She shook her head sadly. "That's just it, Aphra. It's *not* over. Not by a long shot. That's why I can't let you stay. It's not safe for you here."

I laughed bitterly. Not safe? How safe did she think it was sending the Mulos to our island with a paid assassin on their tail? And when I thought about everything I had done to get to Seattle—deceive my dad, ask my best friend Cami to lie for me, deplete my savings—my laughter nearly dissolved into tears.

"Aphra, I wish . . ." I could see the indecision in her eyes. There were things—obviously—she wasn't telling me and it looked like she was trying to decide whether she should.

"Do you know what happened when the Mulos got to the island?" I blurted.

Her face changed immediately and the expression became guarded, wary. "I know some."

"And you still don't know if you can trust me?" I didn't

intend for my voice to sound quite so small or nearly as pathetic, but the words had the intended effect.

"I trust you, Aphra," she said, "but I don't want you to get hurt."

It was a little late for that.

She must have read that thought because she turned in her seat to face me full on and took one of my hands in both of hers. She looked into my eyes, choosing her words very carefully. "Aphra, do you know *why* the Mulos were running?"

I nodded. The Mulos—Seth's family—had once been part of a sleeper cell. Seth's parents defected and offered to help the CIA in exchange for immunity.

"And me?"

"You . . ." I hesitated, lowering my voice, as if anyone could hear us in the van. "You were their contact with the Agency."

She gave me a quick nod. "So you understand the type of people I work with. This is no place for—"

"But I thought you quit."

Her guarded, blank expression returned. "I'm sorry?"

"Seth told me that you left the Agency four years ago." Which happened to be the same time she left my dad and me . . . but I figured it wouldn't be good timing to bring that up.

Her nostrils flared and she took several deep breaths before speaking. "What else did Seth tell you?"

I hesitated for a moment. I didn't mean to get Seth in

trouble—but why should she be angry if all he did was tell me the truth? "He said you suspected that one of the sleepers had infiltrated the Agency. And that when the CIA couldn't—or wouldn't—protect Seth's family, you helped them disappear. But now that they're safe, can't you—"

"Aphra, the Mulos are not the only family in the program who've been compromised. People came forward. They trusted the government. But someone gave them up. Those people must be protected until we can find the identity of the Mole's plant inside the Agency. That's what we've been doing here the past several months—following leads. And the closer we get, the more dangerous it becomes."

We? The guy at the market must be her partner, then. And the pottery business would be their cover. I leaned back against the seat, suddenly very tired. "You're still working for them, aren't you?"

Her voice sounded far away when she spoke. "It's complicated."

I shot her the hardest look I could muster. "Then why don't you uncomplicate it? Either you work for the CIA or you don't."

She searched my eyes for a long moment, hesitating, questioning. Finally, she said, "*Officially*, I quit. I cleared my desk and said my good-byes. But, yes, I still answer to the Agency. Our operation is funded by the Agency. My job is not done, Aphra."

I folded my hands into tight fists and stared, unsee-ing, out the window. What about her job as my mom?

"So you understand why you need to leave? It's much too dangerous for you here. I'll call your dad to meet you in Los Angeles or—"

"Dad can't fly."

Her brows lowered. "What?"

"The doctors won't let Dad travel until he's completely recovered."

"Recovered?"

"From the poison . . . and a minor infection from the tracheotomy. But that wasn't Dr. Mulo's fault. He wasn't exactly working in a sterile environment."

"Jack was poisoned?"

I frowned. "I thought you said you knew what hap-pened on the island."

Her face took on a pinched look that I might have read as genuine concern if I hadn't been so mad at her. "My reports were apparently . . . less than complete."

"He almost died."

She blinked rapidly against the tears glistening in the corner of her eyes. "But he'll recover?"

"Yes."

Her voice cracked as she asked, "Who . . . ?"

"An assassin named Hisako. She was the one trying to kill the Mulos."

"Yes, I knew about her, but I don't understand—"

The cell phone in her pocket buzzed. She flipped it open and barked into the receiver. "What is it?"

As she listened, her expression grew even tighter. She glanced over at me and frowned. "I can't right now. I need to . . . No. Don't go anywhere. I'll be right there."

She snapped her phone shut. "Well, Aphra, it looks like you get your way for now. Something urgent has come up that requires my attention, so I'll need you to come with me. We can talk more tonight."

I sat up straighter, trying not to let my smile show. "Where are we going?" I asked. She didn't answer, but I didn't really care. She wasn't sending me away. Not yet. And I'd take any small victory I could get.

CHAPTER
2

I watched Seattle slip by, the gray-blue water of the sound on one side and the Space Needle rising above the skyline on the other. Ever since I had learned where my mom was living, I'd dreamed about how exciting it was going to be to see those very sights. But now the magic was gone. Everything outside the car windows was just a backdrop.

Mom didn't say a word as we drove. It looked like she was going to once or twice, but she held her tongue. And I held mine. There were so many questions I had to ask her, but I knew I wasn't going to get answers just then.

The road wound through business districts and eclectic neighborhoods before hugging the edge of a massive lake dotted with boats, their white sails puffed full. Under a steel-gray sky, an unseen breeze teased whitecaps on the water. I sat a little straighter, staring at the lake. Already, I missed the ocean back home so much it almost hurt. It was as if I needed to be near water to feel connected. Too soon, buildings and trees obscured the view of the lake, so that all I caught as we zipped past were flashes of blue.

Eventually the van slowed, the turn signal ticking rhythmically, and we turned onto a smaller side street.

"This is where we live," Mom said, gesturing with her chin toward an old four-story apartment building. The architecture was a strange mix of arches, columns, and porticos beneath a flat-top roof.

Mom cleared her throat. "We're . . . subletting, shall we say, while the owner of the apartment is on sabbatical, so we must be careful to maintain a low profile."

"Don't worry," I said. "I'll behave myself."

A wide driveway to one side of the building sloped downward and emptied into a shadowed parking garage beneath the building. A light flickered on as we entered the garage—it must have been on some kind of sensor—but it didn't do much to brighten up the place.

Before Mom had even pulled into her parking spot, a guy who looked to be in his early thirties, with close-cropped hair and horn-rim glasses, rushed toward the van. As we rolled to a stop, he peered into the windows with what I considered to be more than polite curiosity. I stared right back at him. Who was he? I could only guess by Mom's nonreaction at seeing him that she had expected to find the guy waiting there. He probably worked with her, too.

She calmly put the van into park and switched off the ignition while he, on the other hand, fidgeted like he was about to jump out of his skin. He looked like the uptight sort with pressed jeans and a starched oxford shirt buttoned all the way up to the collar. I couldn't see his feet from my vantage point inside the van, but

I could just imagine him wearing polished loafers and dark socks.

Mom told me to stay put and then climbed out to talk to the guy.

"What's going on?" I heard him say before she shut her door. "Where's Joe?"

She and the glasses guy had an animated conversation in front of the van that I couldn't hear. I debated rolling down the window a little so I could eavesdrop, and I might have except that Mom gestured toward the van and the guy's eyes followed her movement. He nodded and walked around to open my door.

"Well, hello." His soft Southern drawl honeyed the words. "It's such a pleasure to meet you."

I swear it was like he was talking to a preschooler. Made me want to hit him. Instead, I mumbled a greeting, hefted my backpack, and climbed out of the van.

He pressed a hand over his chest. "Oh, look at her. She's lovely. This girl is just the spittin' image of you, Nat."

Nat? My mom had always hated people to use that nickname instead of her given name, Natalie. She'd said it made her sound like an annoying insect. But she didn't show any reaction that it bothered her when this guy said it.

He snaked a gentle arm around my shoulder. "All right, darlin'. I s'pose we better go on inside. After that long flight, I'm sure you'll be wanting some rest."

I threw a glance back at my mom, but she was busy unloading a box from the back of the van and didn't look up.

Horn-Rim Glasses Guy guided me toward the stairwell. "I'm Stuart Hunt, by the way." He held out his hand and I automatically shook it, though it seemed like a silly gesture, seeing as his other hand was still draped over my shoulder.

"Aphra Connolly," I mumbled.

"I still can't get over it. Natalie's daughter. Here. It *is* quite a surprise."

He opened the door for me and ushered me inside. The stairwell was painted a vivid blue, and the landing was tiled in a cheerful mosaic pattern. I couldn't help but notice that the tiles themselves looked worn, though, and the grout was stained black and chipped out in several places. A vague odor of turpentine and stale cigarette smoke hung in the air.

"Resident artists," Stuart said, as if he could read my thoughts. "Lots of 'em. Natalie and Joe fit right in with their pottery." His lips pressed together as if hiding a smile. He glanced at my backpack. "I'm afraid it's a rather long climb—we're on the third floor and there's no elevator. May I help you with your . . . luggage?"

"No, thanks," I said quickly. "I've got it."

"Of course." He let the smile spread across his face. "An independent woman. Just like your mother."

I glanced back at Mom, who followed us carrying what

looked like a pretty heavy box. I wondered if Stuart's perception of her as independent kept him from offering to help her with it. I wondered if I should. Offer, I mean.

But then Stuart took my arm and guided me up the steps. "Is this your first time in Seattle?"

"Yes."

"Well, you'll just love it here. It's so . . . eclectic." He smiled, displaying impossibly white, cosmetically perfect teeth. Not that it surprised me. Everything about the guy was fastidious, from his perfectly trimmed hair to his perfectly trimmed fingernails.

When we reached the third-floor landing, he held the door open for me, and—almost as an afterthought, it looked like—for my mom. He ushered me across the hall to a polished wood door with a brass plate tacked in the middle of it that read 307.

"I think you'll be pleased to see where your mother resides," he said. He dug a key from his pocket to unlock the door. "It's actually large by Seattle standards, so we do feel rather fortunate to have found it." He grinned in a way that made me think fortune had little to do with it.

The place wasn't luxurious by any means. Not that I was being a snob, but it was a far cry from the resort—even the employees' quarters. But it was clean. Obsessively so. Even the couch cushions were symmetrically arranged. I eyed Stuart's proud smile and knew immediately who was responsible for that touch.

"It's very nice," I murmured.

"Why, thank you." He beamed. "But you haven't even seen the best part yet. Come on back. I'll show you."

"She doesn't need a tour, Stuart," Mom said.

"Nonsense." He ignored her and led me down a long hallway. "All the bedrooms are along this hall," he said. "Except for this here." He tapped the door and it gave a hollow thunk. "This is the commode . . . and a shower, in case you'd like to freshen up a bit." He eyed my travel-crumpled shorts and T-shirt with a pained expression. "But first"—he opened another door grandly to reveal a tiny room at the end of the hallway—"this is the study. It has a lake view. Come see."

I followed him out a set of sliding doors to a small overhang that he called the balcony. There wasn't even enough room out there to put a chair or anything. More accurately, it was the small landing of what looked like a fire escape. A narrow ladder to the side of the balcony stretched up past other balconies and down, I supposed, to the ground.

Stuart directed my attention once again. "You have to lean out a bit to see the water. See, look. Over there. That's Lake Union."

"That down there?" I pointed to the water I could see beyond the trees that stood behind the building.

"No, no. That's part of the Ballard locks. Those locks connect Lake Union to Salmon Bay and eventually the sound. Like a ship canal, you understand? But that . . ." He leaned even farther out and pointed toward the corner of the building. "*That* is Lake Union."

I appropriately "ahhed" at the small patch of grayish water. Really, I couldn't see enough of it to be truly impressed.

He stepped back, satisfied.

Just then, a gruff man's voice demanded, "What is *she* doing here?"

I jumped and spun around to find Joe in the doorway, glaring at me like I was the devil incarnate.

"I didn't have a chance yet to get her to the airport," Mom said.

"So you brought her *here*?"

She stared him down. "Not now, Joe."

Mom must have been his senior because he clamped his mouth shut, following orders. To a point. He may not have used words, but the look in his eyes spoke volumes. He was not happy.

She nodded toward the front room. "Let's get started."

Stuart bowed to me. Seriously. He actually bowed! "If you'll excuse me. Duty calls."

I looked to Mom, but she had already turned away and was following Joe down the hall. Stuart left the room and closed the door behind him. The signal was clear. I was to stay out of the way while they did whatever it was covert CIA agents did.

I shook my head. *Come see the view.* Yeah. Right. Get the kid to the back room where she won't be a bother was more like it. Stuart's Southern-gentleman act was effective, I'd give him that. I might have laughed at his clever manipulation if I wasn't just a little bit peeved. Okay, more than a little. I didn't like being duped.

I tiptoed over to the door, half expecting it to be locked, but the handle turned easily in my hand. Slowly, I cracked the door open just enough to see the three of them at the end of the narrow hallway, heads bent together around the kitchen table, an open laptop before them.

"Look at the coordinates," Stuart was saying. "This could be it."

"Verified?" Mom asked.

"Not yet. I can put a call in to—"

Mom laid a hand on his arm and he stopped. "Aphra," she said, "could you close the door, please?"

I pulled back, face burning. I clicked the door shut and stood staring at it. In that instant, I was a little kid again, caught spying on the grown-ups. I wasn't one of them. I didn't belong with them. I shook my head to clear it of that thought. I *did* belong with my mom. Didn't I? Just not at that moment.

I stood hugging my arms. The room began to feel very small. Confining. I paced. For the record, it took only four long strides to cover the entire length. Before long, I began to feel claustrophobic.

I pushed back out onto the little "balcony." At least I could breathe out there. Leaning out over the railing, I peered at the little patch of visible lake. It was hardly worth the effort. I folded my arms, resting my elbows on the railing, and blew out a breath. What was I supposed to do for the next however-long?

"Nice morning, huh?"

I had been leaning out to the right to see the lake and hadn't noticed that there was a guy on the next balcony to the left. He had a tall, lean frame and, judging by the smoothness of his face, couldn't have been much older than me. The sun-bleached tips of his tousled mocha hair seemed to catch the light when he moved. Dark eyebrows raised in question over deep brown eyes. He smiled and I swear it was like the sun had broken through the clouds.

I realized my mouth was hanging open and closed it. "I'm sorry," I managed. "I didn't realize anyone was out here."

His smile broadened. "No worries."

I stood there, feeling awkward and obvious, and ran my hand down the front of my shorts, smoothing out the wrinkles. Suddenly I wished that I had taken Stuart's suggestion to freshen up.

"I haven't seen you around before," he said. "Are you new?"

"Oh. I'm . . ." I shuffled my feet and reached for the comfort of the chain around my neck that held Seth's ring. "I'm just here visiting my mom."

"Well, welcome to the neighborhood." He stretched his arm across the space separating the balconies. "I'm Ryan, by the way."

I shook his hand. His grip was firm and his rough skin warm. I swallowed and pulled my hand back. Why was my mouth suddenly so dry? "I'm Aphra," I croaked.

"So, Aphra, how do you like Seattle?"

I said, "It's nice," and then groaned inside. What an insipid answer!

"How long will you be with us?"

"I—I'm not really sure."

He leaned casually against the railing. "I know what you mean. I'm a part-timer myself."

"Part-timer?"

"Yeah, I work the salmon season up in Ketchikan to pay for school. I only come down here to make deliveries."

"What school do you go to?"

He grinned. "UW Seattle, where else? Go Huskies!"

"Oh. So . . . do you take a boat to Ketchikan, or . . ."

His laugh danced in the air between us. "Are you kidding? No way. I fly." Then he glanced at the ladder and back at me. "Have you been up to the roof yet?"

I followed his gaze. "Um, no."

"You've got to go up there. Great view . . . although there's not much to see this morning; it's too overcast. On a clear day, we have a pretty spectacular view of Mount Ranier."

"I hope I can see it sometime." And I meant it, too. I hoped my mom would let me stay long enough.

"You can see the lake from up there. And my plane."

"Oh?"

"Yeah. Come on. I'll show you." He hoisted himself up onto the railing and then out onto the ladder in one smooth motion, pausing just a second to turn and look back down at me. "Do you need help?"

Was he kidding? I'd been rock climbing since I was ten. I'd even climbed a trellis or two. "I've got it."

I followed him up the ladder, pushing aside the little uneasy quells that said my mom wouldn't be happy to find me gone from the room. But if she was going to ignore me, what did she expect? Plus, come on. Like I wasn't going to follow this guy.

Ryan reached back from the top and offered his hand to help me up the last few rungs and onto the roof. This time I accepted his offer. He pulled me up, and it could just be wishful thinking, but I'm pretty sure he held on to my hand longer than was absolutely necessary.

I had to admit, the view was much more impressive from the roof than it had been from the balcony. Lake Union stretched out to one side, the water gray blue under the haze of clouds. "It's beautiful."

"Just wait until the clouds burn off," Ryan said. "You won't believe the view." He crossed to the far side of the roof and leaned against the half wall. I followed as if magnetically linked with him.

"There's my baby," he said, beckoning to me.

I was already right next to him, but I couldn't help it. I took another step forward. He leaned close, nearly touching his face to mine, and wrapped an arm around my shoulders. "Look down there, you see those docks?" He pointed down to the lake and the motion pulled me even closer. "The second one from the end. You see that plane?"

I did. Just the top of it.

"That's mine."

"Cool."

"Well, actually, it's my family's, but I fly it when I'm working."

He flashed another smile and my stomach flip-flopped. I pulled away and crossed to the other side of the roof. He followed, chatting easily about the joys of flying and how he'd gotten his pilot's license through the Civil Air Patrol when he was just sixteen. I hardly heard his words because of the alarm bells suddenly clanging inside my head.

I'm not quite sure why it took so long for me to come to my senses. Maybe because I was hungry for some normal conversation. Maybe because I was enjoying his proximity so much. But I knew my mom wouldn't be happy about me risking her cover, sneaking about and making contact with her neighbors—even polite, charming, and exceedingly good-looking neighbors.

I backed toward the ladder. "Um . . . I should probably go. It was nice meeting you."

"Yeah. You, too." He gave me one last dazzling smile. "I'll see you around."

I'll admit to being more than just a little disappointed that he stayed on the roof instead of climbing back down with me, but what did I expect? He probably thought I was a stupid little girl who had to get home before her mommy got mad. And he would be right.

After my rooftop encounter, there was no way I could stay confined in the tiny room. I grabbed my backpack and tapped on the door before opening it. Mom, Stuart, and Joe stared at me from the kitchen table.

"Excuse me," I said. "Would it bother you if I took a quick shower? I don't think I can stand these clothes a minute longer."

They exchanged glances. Stuart shrugged. Joe scowled. Finally, Mom gave me a brief nod. "Yes, of course. Go ahead."

I thanked them and padded down the hall to what Stuart had called the commode—a term I hadn't heard since my dad and I left South Carolina years before.

Even in the bathroom, Stuart's fixation with order was evident in the way the towels were folded over the bar and the rubber shower mat was aligned at right angles to the wall. More color-coordinated towels were stacked neatly, square in the center of the toilet tank, and a bottle of hand soap had been perfectly placed on the back corner of the sink.

I grabbed my clean clothes from my backpack and stripped out of my old ones, stuffing them into a plastic bag I had brought for that purpose. The chain holding Seth's ring came off next, and I zipped it securely into a little outer pocket of my backpack before stepping under the water.

I suppose I took a leisurely shower; I wasn't really keeping track. All I knew was that my options within the apartment were severely limited and I preferred the feel of warm water drizzling over my head to the claustrophobia of the back room. I didn't think I took *that* long, though, so I was more than a little bit taken aback when someone started pounding on the door. I still had to rinse my hair.

"Just a minute!" I called.

"Hurry up!"

I could tell by the cranky tone that it was Joe. I almost wanted to take longer just to spite him, but I knew that would have been childish. Satisfying, but childish. I don't know what I had done to make him dislike me so much, but it was clear he did. And, in turn, that didn't endear him to me.

Still, I wanted to keep the peace with my mom, so I hurried to finish my shower. I had barely turned off the water when he pounded again. What was his problem? I toweled off as quickly as I could and wiggled, still damp, into my clothes. All I could do with my hair was pull it back into a quick ponytail.

I opened the door and Joe nearly fell into the bathroom. He must have been leaning on it from the other
side. I gasped and stepped back, but he grabbed my
arm and yanked me out of the room. "About time," he
growled, and pushed past me into the bathroom.

"Wait." I reached out to stop the door from closing.
"Just let me get my—"

Slam!

I turned to complain to my mom, but she and Stuart
stood at the kitchen counter now, furiously discussing
something in low, agitated voices. I edged closer.

". . . every day in the same exact place," Stuart was saying. "I know when something has been moved."

Mom shook her head. "I understand, Stuart. But that
doesn't mean—"

"No? Well look at this." Stuart turned the screen of his
laptop toward her. "You know I monitor everything that
comes in and out of this place, right? I even put tracking
code in my own computer, which he must not have been
counting on."

"What are you talking about?"

"This." Stuart tapped the screen. "It's Langley. He sent
them a message last night."

It wasn't until that moment that Mom even noticed
I was standing there. "Aphra, I'll be with you in a
moment."

I gestured back toward the bathroom. "But my—"

Her look silenced me. I shuffled—as slowly as I could—down the hallway, but I didn't need to worry; she had already forgotten me. I leaned against the wall just out of her line of vision and listened.

"What did it say?" she whispered to Stuart.

"I don't know. It was encrypted and it will take me a while to work it out. But look . . . the same office, two days ago. And this"—I could hear him tap the computer screen—"last week. He's been in constant contact with someone in that office. Why? What isn't he telling us?"

Mom made a disbelieving sound. I don't know if she was denying it was true or if she just didn't want to accept it. "He could be talking with an old friend. Joe was with the Agency for over twenty years; he's got a lot of colleagues."

Stuart's voice sounded peeved. "Okay, if you say so. You're the boss."

"I'm sure it's fine," she assured him. I hadn't been around long enough to be the best judge, but to me, her confidence sounded forced.

Joe came out of the bathroom then, in as foul a mood as he'd entered. Mom and Stuart fell silent and didn't even respond while Joe griped and complained. Whatever it was the three of them had been discussing before, Joe was obviously not very happy about it.

"You two do what you want," he snapped. "I'm going back to the Market. In case you have forgotten, Natalie, we have a scheduled contact today. One of us should be there." With that, he grabbed the keys from the counter and slammed out the door.

Stuart shot a meaningful look at my mom, but she studiously ignored him. Despite her outward calm, though, I could practically feel the tension building, filling the room.

I realized once again that the timing of my visit had been supremely bad. But I couldn't have known. It wasn't my fault. At least, that's what I tried desperately to believe.

CHAPTER
3

After Joe slammed out of the apartment, no one moved or spoke for a full minute. Mom finally broke the silence. "I checked with the airlines," she said, glancing up at me. "There aren't any direct flights until six."

So she had been aware that I was still standing there. I wasn't sure whether to act chagrined or innocent. "Um, okay." A six-o'clock flight meant I wouldn't have to be to the airport until four-thirty or five. At least I'd get to spend part of the day with my mom.

Or not. Stuart moved his laptop closer to her. "That will give us just about enough time to go over these witness statements." He gave me an apologetic smile. "It'll only take a moment. You don't mind, do you, darlin'?"

Of course I minded. And I hoped Mom did, too. I waited for her to say something, but her eyes flicked over to whatever was on Stuart's screen and she didn't give me a second thought.

I grabbed my backpack from the bathroom and retreated to the study. I threw the backpack on a chair and paced back and forth, the frustration building inside me until I wanted to scream. But all that would probably accomplish was for me to get dropped at the airport early. I wasn't really mad at Stuart, although for someone who was so well mannered, it was a pretty insensitive move to interject himself and the work like that. But it was my mom I was truly upset with. We had only a little while before we had to get ready to go to the airport. She'd been gone for four years; couldn't she give me even a couple of hours?

And what was I supposed to do until she was ready for me? There was nothing to do in the room. It felt like a cage. A very small, very boring cage.

I pushed out the door to the balcony, but even that felt too confining. At least the sky had cleared.

That thought was quickly followed by the memory of Ryan saying how the view from the roof was so spectacular on clear days. And that thought was followed by the picture of him leaning close, pointing out his seaplane among the boats and planes at the docks. Heat crept up my face. I had to admit it would be pleasant seeing him again—if only to say good-bye. I wondered if he would still be up there.

It didn't take long to decide what I was going to do. I slipped back into the room and crossed to the door. I opened it a crack. Mom and Stuart were still busily discussing whatever it was she wanted me out of the room for. I closed the door quietly and depressed the lock. Just in case.

Back out on the balcony, I quickly climbed to the top before I could change my mind.

I have to admit I was disappointed to find the rooftop deserted. I sighed. At least the view was worth the climb. I turned slowly, drinking it in. It was just as Ryan had described, only better. On one side of the building and down from the locks lay the lake, the sun winking across the surface and changing the color from a slate gray to a deep cerulean blue. On the other, the white dome of Mount Rainier rose from beyond the city. I couldn't believe how close it looked.

"I *thought* that was you."

I jumped and spun around. "Oh! Ryan. Hi."

He gave me one of his easy grins and I couldn't help but smile back. He crossed the roof to stand next to me and leaned his elbows on the railing. "Turned out to be a perfect day, huh? One of only about sixty sunny days for the year."

"It's beautiful," I murmured. And it was. Beautiful, that is. But it wasn't perfect. Not by a long shot.

"Enjoy it while it lasts. We're supposed to get rain tomorrow."

My smile faded. Not because of the rain, but because if Mom had her way, I wouldn't be there to see it. "Oh."

"Yeah. I'm supposed to make a run in the morning, but I think I'll take off tonight before the weather gets here. After the Mariners game, of course."

"Of course."

"Ah. You a Mariners fan?"

"Uh . . ." I had never actually seen a baseball game in

my life, but that didn't stop me from saying, "Sure, when-ever I'm in Seattle."

He laughed and I joined him, but my laugh sounded high-pitched and phony to my ears. What was I doing? I didn't even know this guy. Why was I flirting with him? He was in college and he flew a plane. I was just a child com-pared to him. And then, of course, there was Seth . . .

I quickly sobered. "I should go in. I just wanted to see this one more time."

He cocked his head and frowned. "I guess I'll see you around then."

"Yeah." I stepped a foot onto the ladder. "I'll see you."

He said good-bye and turned his back on me to wan-der back over to the railing. I climbed downward, feeling a little hurt and a lot stupid.

At least the distraction gave me time to think. I made a decision; I wasn't going to sit around in the room any-more—well, okay, since I had climbed to the roof and back, I really hadn't been sitting around, and I didn't intend to. If Mom had things to do, she could go ahead and do them. With me.

I swung my backpack up onto my shoulder and marched to the door, not being careful to open it quietly this time. I strode down the hall.

Stuart nudged her when I walked into the kitchen. She gave me a look—not really startled, but not alto-gether composed, either. "We don't have to leave for a few minutes, Aphra."

"I know." I settled into one of the kitchen chairs. "I got bored back there."

"Well, of course you did, darlin'," Stuart said; gushing. "I'm sorry; I wasn't thinking. Nat, perhaps we should finish this later. I think Aphra wants to spend some time with you."

He was right. About me wanting to spend time with my mom, I mean. But it still bugged me when he said it like I was some little baby wanting her mama. Not half as much as it bugged me the way Mom sighed and shut down her computer, though. She acted like it was some kind of chore that she had to figure out what to do with me until she could dump me at the airport.

She stood. "Are you hungry, Aphra? We could go grab something to eat before your flight."

"Sure," I said halfheartedly. Now I felt like a petulant little kid who was getting her way only because she'd thrown a tantrum.

"Well, grab your things. Let's—"

"Wait." Stuart held up a hand. "Nat, you better come look at this."

She crossed to his side of the counter and stood next to him, staring at his computer. "What is this?"

"This right here is Joe." He tapped the screen.

"You put a *tracking device* on the van?"

He looked insulted. "I put a tracking device on *all* the vehicles. How else would I know how to find you if something happened?"

"He's in the city. So what?"

"He said he was going to the Market. What's he doing on the other side of town?"

"Maybe he had errands. I don't see how this is any of your—"

"But he said he—"

"Let it go, Stuart. I'm going to take my daughter out now. Are you going to track *me*?"

Stuart sulked and went back to staring at the computer screen. He didn't even say good-bye when we left.

Well, no wonder Mom had grown moody; she worked with a couple of prima donnas. "I don't know how you can stand it," I said.

She paused, one hand on the stairwell door. "Stand what?"

"Stuart. And Joe. What's with them?"

She pursed her lips for a second and then ushered me down the stairs. "There's a lot you don't understand, Aphra."

"So you keep saying."

Mom paused and regarded me for a moment. "You're right. I think it's time you were enlightened. But not here. We'll talk in the car."

The garage light clicked on as soon as she opened the door. Compared to the bright colors and artistic touches inside the building, the garage felt sad and bleak. Just the perfect setting for a heartfelt mother–daughter talk, I thought dismally.

Mom cut across the garage, past a chain-link compound crowded with kayaks and locked-up bicycles, toward a small blue sedan parked in the corner. She pressed a button on her key fob and the horn chirped, lights flashed. That would be our ride, then.

I looked around the garage for the van, but I didn't see it. Joe must have taken it. Personally, I would have chosen the car if I were him, but I was more than happy to swap vehicles. As looks go, the car was about as unremarkable as the van, but it was obviously newer and probably more comfortable.

I opened the back door and threw my backpack onto the seat and then climbed into the front.

"Put your seat belt on," Mom said automatically. I almost laughed. Or would have, if I didn't feel so much like crying. Sad as it was, that was the first motherly thing she had said to me since I had gotten to Seattle—now that I was leaving.

She stuck the keys into the ignition, but she didn't start the engine. For a long moment she just sat, looking out over the steering wheel—at what, I don't know.

"Joe, Stuart, and I work together for a reason," Mom said, "but none of us chose the assignment." She traced the pattern of the leather grip on the steering wheel. "Each of us has a history with the Mole. I was in charge of protecting the woman who sent him to jail. Joe ran the task force that gathered evidence against him. Stuart hacked into an online crime ring the Mole had orchestrated while he was in prison."

When she raised her eyes to me, I was struck by the pain I saw in them. And scared.

"Once he escaped from prison, the Mole swore to take revenge, and he hit where it would hurt most. Joe lost his wife. Stuart's parents were murdered." She paused, letting the information sink in. "I am the only one who hasn't lost someone, Aphra, and I'd like to keep it that way. Do you understand why you need to stay far away from me? In the meantime, I can put up with a little surliness from the boys. They've earned the right to be moody."

She turned the key then, and the engine hummed to life. I couldn't say anything, but just stared at her as she carefully backed the car out of the spot. She might as well have backed over my chest. I wished that I could take my words back. I wished that I could play the day over and be a little more understanding. I wished that she had told me in the first place.

She shifted the car into drive and gave me a long look before pulling out of the garage. "I'm sorry that I had to keep this from you. I know you think I chose my job over you, but you are and always will be my first priority. Until we know where the Mole is hiding and who his operatives are within the Agency, I figured that the less you knew, the better. I thought it might keep you from becoming a target."

"Then why did you send the Mulos to our resort?" The words slipped out before I could stop them.

A small sigh escaped her lips, tinged with regret. "It was a bad call. I thought we had covered their tracks. I thought no one would find them."

"You didn't know," I murmured, anxious to salve the guilt I saw in her face.

"No, but I should have." She turned the corner and I realized we were passing the lake again, on our way back toward the city. "In my mind, you were still twelve. My little girl. I should have known better than to send a teenage boy to the island. And now . . ."

"Now what?"

"Now you're on the radar." She slid a sad look at me. "They'll watch you, hoping Seth will contact you. And now that you've left the island, they will want to know where you are going and why."

"Hold on. What are you talking about? Who's 'they'?"

"The Agency. And possibly . . . others."

"But . . ."

"Why do you think I stayed away all those years? I didn't want to draw attention to where you were."

"What about the cards? You sent me cards."

For the first time she smiled. Well, almost. Her lips curved upward, but her eyes were still sad. "I'm glad you got them. I never knew."

I decided not to tell her how Dad had kept them from

me and that I had only found where he had hidden them a couple of months ago. There's nothing either of us could do about that.

"What were the flowers on the back? Every one of them had a flower."

Her eyes misted as she looked at me. "You noticed them? Those were myosotis. You know, forget-me-nots? Corny, I know, but at the Swiss resort where your father and I honeymooned, the things grew everywhere. I loved them, but Jack said they were like weeds; you couldn't kill them. I . . . I wanted to give him a sign that I was still okay."

"And the postmarks?" I asked. "They were from all over the place."

"Yes. We've had to keep moving. Seattle has been our longest stopover, and we've only been here about four months. But we should probably move on now . . ."

She didn't say much else. She didn't have to; I could read the tension in her hunched-up shoulders and her death grip on the steering wheel.

I slid down in the seat, feeling like a complete idiot. All this time, the only one I had been thinking about was myself, worrying about how *I* felt, what *I* wanted. And now I had caused Mom more worry and compromised her operation. I should have listened to the part of me that said the Seattle trip wasn't a good idea. I should have stayed at home where I belonged.

●●●

We were halfway to the airport when Mom's cell phone buzzed. She grabbed it from her pocket and flipped it open, glancing at the screen before answering. "Where are you?" Pause. "And you didn't think that it would be a good idea to tell me before you rushed off?" Pause. "No, I cannot come to your—" Her grip on the phone tightened. "What? No, tell me now." She listened and her face went white. "I understand," she said in a deliberately neutral voice. "I need to deliver the package and then I will meet you."

The package. Me. I was keeping her from doing her job. "Mom—"

She cut me off with a shake of her head. "Half hour. Maybe forty-five minutes." Pause. "Of course you can wait! Stay where you are."

I nudged her arm. "You can go *now*. I'm in no hurry."

She seemed to be considering it as she slid a glance at me, but then she shook her head and cupped her hand over the phone to whisper to me, "No. I need to get you out of here."

"Mom. I can wait in the car. Don't worry; I won't get in the way."

She hesitated only for a second, but that was enough. I understood a lot in that instant. I was a burden, an extra worry—and she didn't need any more of those.

"Really," I said. "Do what you need to do."

The relief on her face was clear. "I'll be right there,"

she said into the phone. She snapped it shut and swerved into the outside lane. We took the next exit and doubled back toward the city.

I pretended to be watching out the window, blinking fast to keep the tears in check. All I had hoped for and waited for these past years was to be with my mom. Unfortunately, my timing sucked. Maybe once she had found the answers she was looking for, there would be time for us. Until then, I needed to keep out of her hair.

I knew what I had to do. When Mom went looking for Joe, I would find my own way back to the airport.

I recognized the area near the Market as we drove toward the crowded parking lot under the freeway. Had I really just left there that morning? I saw the van parked next to one of the pillars. Joe must be close. Mom pulled into one of the last remaining vacant spots and switched off the engine. For a long while she just sat and stared out the windshield. Her frown told me she was unsure again.

"Go," I insisted. "I'll be fine."

She looked at me with unreadable eyes. I couldn't tell what it was that she was trying to hide. Regret, maybe? "Lock the doors," she said. "Stay low."

I assured her that I would. And I planned to. Stay low, that is. I just wouldn't be doing it inside the car.

She hadn't been gone more than a minute when a taxi rolled by, headed up the hill. I jumped from the car to flag it down, slamming the door behind me. Too late, I remembered the automatic locks. My backpack was inside the car. All my money, my ID, everything else was inside the car as well. I pounded my hand against the window and rattled the door handle. How could I have been so stupid?

I noticed some people a couple of rows down, casting curious looks in my direction. So much for laying low. I stopped pounding and stepped back. What I should not be doing was attracting attention.

Hugging my arms, I glanced around the parking lot. There were at least a dozen people walking through the lot, either coming or going. Obviously, I couldn't just stand around waiting for my mom to come back. They might think I was casing the lot to break into cars or something.

Maybe I could wait in the van. I rushed over and jiggled the door handles, just in case Joe had left it open. He hadn't.

There were plenty of shops nearby and I supposed I could hide out in one of them, but no matter where I went, I would eventually have to explain to my mom why I hadn't done as I had promised. I slumped against the van and looked down the street in the direction she had gone. I should probably hang out in one of the shops along that route so I could see her return. At least that way she wouldn't get back to the car and find me gone.

Then I saw her. Well, just her head, really, but she

had stopped only a block or so away with the cell phone pressed against one ear and her hand pressed against the other.

As if she could feel me looking at her, she glanced back at the parking lot. I ducked behind the van again, unable to shake the feeling that something was wrong. Besides me being locked out of the car, I mean. It was the way she was frowning, her brows in a worried bunch over her eyes. The whole time I had been with her, she'd been careful to keep her face impassive, completely expressionless. Either she'd let her guard down just then because she didn't think anyone was watching . . . or something was up.

When I dared peek around the van, I saw her hurrying down the sidewalk, away from me. On impulse, I decided to follow her. I knew I shouldn't. I knew she'd be mad, but I couldn't just sit there. Not after that look I'd seen on her face. I couldn't imagine what I could possibly do to help, but if she was in trouble, I had to give it a try.

I rushed to the street corner and pummeled the cross-walk button. The red hand kept flashing as she walked farther and farther away. I couldn't wait. I bolted across the street. A Nissan coming down the hill screeched to a stop, horn blaring. The driver yelled something at me, but I didn't have the patience to listen. I raced after my mom.

I lost her in the crowd by the end of the second block. She must have turned up a side street or gone into a store or something because one moment I saw the back of her head and the next she was gone. I planted my hands on my hips and tried to catch my breath as I turned in a slow circle, looking for any sign of her.

That's when I saw Joe. He was sitting at a little table in front of a sidewalk café, checking his watch and looking around as if he was waiting for someone.

So where was my mom?

A waiter in a long green apron stepped over to Joe and set an oversize cup on the table. Joe barely looked up. He checked his watch again and reached absently for the cup, raising it to his lips to take a sip. Abruptly, his expression changed. He made a bitter face and set the cup down so quickly that coffee and froth sloshed onto the white tablecloth. Frowning, he raised his fingers to wipe away the foam that clung to his upper lip and then stared at the residue. He sniffed his fingers, brows dropping tight and low. His frown deepened. With a quick glance back toward the café, he tried to stand, but dropped heavily back onto his chair.

The whole thing probably took only a couple seconds, but it played like a bad dream, everything unfolding in slow motion. He raised a hand to his throat, a mixture of confusion and anger crossing his face as his eyes bulged wide and his mouth hung open. And then he began to make choking noises.

Back home on the island, I had been certified as a lifeguard. My training taught me to react quickly and

analyze later. Seeing Joe struggle to breathe kicked me
into autopilot. If I had taken the time to think, I might
not have run toward him. I might have considered that
someone was trying to kill the guy and it would do well
for me to lay low. But I wasn't thinking. I raced to where
he had fallen onto the sidewalk and dropped to my knees
beside him.

"Joe? Can you hear me?" He was still clawing at his
neck and I had to hit his hands away so I could loosen
his collar. "Are you getting any air?" I asked, fighting to
keep my voice steady.

"The . . . latte . . ." he wheezed.

Well, at least he was breathing. I pressed my fingers to
the side of his neck. His pulse was going crazy.

He grabbed my hand. "In . . . the . . ." His words were
lost in a spasm of coughing. "The . . . list . . ."

"Try to relax."

"Cup . . . hold . . . c-c-up . . . ho-holder . . ." Suddenly his
eyes rolled back and his head jerked like someone had
yanked a string at the top of his skull. His grip squeezed
like a vise around my hand. I yelped and pried my fingers free.

At the same moment a hand grabbed my shoulder. "Aphra!" Mom's voice hissed. "What are you doing
here?"

"He's . . . he's . . ."

"You can't get mixed up in this!" She yanked me to my
feet. "Get back to the car. Go!"

She gave me a push and I stumbled through the crowd of people who had begun to gather around Joe's table.

A lady plucked at my arm. "What happened? Do you know that man?"

I rubbed my sore fingers and looked back to where Mom had bent over Joe, her eyes pinched with concern. "No," I said flatly. "I've never seen him before."

CHAPTER 4

I knew I was supposed to leave, but I couldn't pull my eyes from Joe's body thrashing on the sidewalk. My mom grabbed his head to keep him from smacking it on the cement, but there wasn't much else she could do for him. Only the waiter and one other man stepped forward to see if they could help. Everyone else hovered at a safe distance, watching. They acted as if they were at a Saturday matinee or something.

Mom looked to the waiter. "He's seizing. Grab a table-cloth to cushion his head!" Then to the man, "You. Call 911!"

The man whipped a cell phone from his pocket and stabbed at the numbers while the waiter yanked a table-cloth free of the nearest table. He bunched it up and shoved it under Joe's head so that my mom could let go.

The lady standing next to me wrung her hands. "What's wrong? Shouldn't they put something in his mouth? Why aren't they helping him?"

I ignored her and stared straight ahead.

Just then Joe stopped convulsing. His body arched one last time and then he lay deathly still.

"Sir?" Mom leaned close, pressing two fingers against the side of his neck. "Sir, can you hear me?" I could see the answer pass over her face before she let it go blank again. "He needs some air!" she yelled at the crowd. "Clear out!"

A few people took a step back, but most of them were glued to their spots. There was no way they were leaving the show. Mom started CPR, even though I'm pretty sure she knew it wouldn't do any good. As she was starting chest compressions, Joe's head lolled to the side, his eyes open but empty. My stomach lurched and I looked away.

In the distance, a siren wailed. The sound sent a quiver of fear through my belly. I'm not sure why. I hadn't done anything wrong . . . unless you counted the part where I came to Seattle uninvited, interrupted the work my mom and her colleagues were doing, and wandered into a crime scene.

I backed away from the crowd. I should have listened to Mom when she told me to go. I should never have come in the first place.

"Hey, miss," a woman in the crowd called. "Miss! Where are you going?"

I didn't turn back but walked quickly away from the scene. I wanted to run, but if I had learned anything from watching Mom, it was to not draw attention to myself. I walked down the sidewalk, outwardly calm, and tried to adapt my mom's bland expression even though I was screaming inside.

It took such concentration to keep the emotion from

my face that I had gone a couple of blocks before I noticed a man on the other side of the street who seemed to be matching my stride, mirroring my movements. I probably wouldn't have noticed him at all except that I caught a reflection of him in a store window. He seemed to be staring straight at me. I paused and pretended to admire something inside the store so that I could get a better look at him, but he bent his blond head away from me and stooped to tie his shoelace.

He was definitely following me. Why? And then I thought about it. I had interrupted Joe's murder. I had touched him, spoken to him. Whoever killed him might think Joe had told me something I shouldn't know. Something worth killing for. The idea brought with it a cold panic that coiled around my throat so tightly I could hardly breathe.

What should I *do*? I couldn't lead the guy to the car. I couldn't go back to the café, either. I wanted to yell, to scream, but instead I made myself stroll casually past the next shop, a vacant smile plastered on my face. Meanwhile, my mind raced. Mom would have been more aware of her surroundings. She would have already mapped out an escape route. I would have to improvise.

I took quick note of the people around me: a couple of guys in shirtsleeves, a cluster of touristy-looking types talking in loud voices, a lady walking a big black dog. It wasn't likely that the guy would do anything in front of all those people, so maybe he was just watching me.

I stood at the crosswalk next to the shirtsleeve guys, waiting for the light to change. From the corner of my eye, I watched as the man waited at the crosswalk on his side of the road. The light turned green. I stepped down from the curb. Across the street, he did the same. I took a couple of steps forward, but as soon as the cars started moving through the intersection, I spun, jumped back onto the sidewalk, and ran for the nearest store.

I didn't stop to see if he was coming after me. I just hoped that he wouldn't try to cut through the traffic, and that I'd have a minute-or-so head start.

A hanging bell jangled when I yanked open the door, and I dashed into what looked like some kind of New Age gift boutique. Inside, a cloying smell of incense weighted the stagnant air. Racks of crystal jewelry, dream catchers, and bottles of essential oils lined one wall and a wrought-iron staircase ascended along the other. Breathy flute music played softly in the background. My footsteps creaked across the aged wooden floor, but the lady behind the counter didn't even look up. She licked her thumb and turned a page in the magazine she was reading.

I cleared my throat. "Excuse me. Do you have a restroom?"

She gave me a brief, bored glance and pointed to the stairs. "Captain Nemo's. Up the stairs on the left."

I thanked her and took the stairs two at a time. On the second floor, the glass front of Captain Nemo's pub dominated the left-hand wall. Through the soles of my feet, I could feel the vibration of the heavy bass music inside. The bar was crowded with what looked like an after-work crowd. I could probably lose myself in there.

But then I saw something better. At the end of the hallway stood an emergency exit. I ran for the door and slipped through it just as I heard the bell downstairs jangle again.

I cringed at every footfall as I rushed down the stairs, every movement echoing through the bare cement stairwell. Because of the way the building was situated at the bottom of a steep hill, the exterior exit was only half a flight down. I set my sights on the door and tried to tread as lightly as I could. I had nearly reached it when the door on the first floor burst open.

"Hey!" a man's voice yelled. "Stop!"

I didn't care about noise anymore. I crashed out the metal exterior door and into the alleyway behind the building. Garbage bins and empty boxes filled the alley. Something sour leaked from one of the bins and snaked along the downward slope toward the building. I recoiled from the stench and ran the other way.

I didn't have to turn around to know he was behind me. I heard the exterior door bang open before I even reached the end of the block. I turned and pounded down a faded wooden staircase and tore through a narrow alleyway between two tall buildings. Back on the sidewalk again, I wiped the expression from my face and jogged to the corner. From there, I cut up the street to a path that wound through a miniature park.

As I tore down the path, I caught the flash of red lights through the trees to my left. My feet slowed and then stumbled to a stop as I realized that the café lay just below the park. Through the branches, I could see the round tables with their crisp white tablecloths. An ambulance idled at the curb as two paramedics draped a sheet over a figure lying on the gurney. The waiter was talking to a policeman, who was writing things down in a notebook. There was no sign of Mom.

She must have slipped away. Which meant she was probably heading back to the car. Where she would look for me. And I wouldn't be there.

I needed to get back to the parking lot, but I needed to be sure I lost my tail first. How, I wasn't sure, but I didn't have time to think about it. From behind me came the sound of running feet. I spun and bolted up the park's grassy hill to the street above. When I reached the sidewalk, I banked right. At the bottom of the hill ran the raised freeway—my only familiar landmark. As long as I made sure I could see the freeway, I would be able to find my way back to the parking lot.

I ducked into the first doorway I came to and pressed my back against the wall, praying that the man hadn't seen which way I had gone. I held my breath, waiting, hoping, resisting a quick peek around the corner to see if he was coming. One moment passed, then another and another. It seemed logical that if he had seen where I'd gone, he would have passed the doorway by then. I made myself wait a little longer just to be sure. Nothing.

Cautiously, I pulled myself away from the wall and peered down the sidewalk. It was empty. I didn't celebrate too much, though. If he had followed the path through the park instead of cutting through the trees, it wouldn't take him long to discover I hadn't gone that way, and he might come looking for me.

At one end of the block, I saw a whole group of people crossing the street, laughing, talking. More than the usual neighborhood foot traffic. I figured it would be easier to lose myself in a crowd, so I chased after them. Once I was sure he wasn't following me anymore, I'd find my way back to the car. I just hoped my mom would still be there.

By the time I reached the corner, they were halfway up the hill. I ran to join them—which turned out to be much harder than I had imagined it would be because of the angle of the hill. By the time I reached the tail end of their group, I was wheezing like a smoker with asthma.

I watched the hill below me. Nothing. Perfect. Mingling with the other pedestrians, I crossed the street. I had no idea where they all were going, but I did know there was safety in numbers. As long as I was surrounded by people, my pursuer would likely keep his distance.

Faint strains of reggae music drifted down the sidewalk and grew louder as I walked. Bright banners in

LINDA GERBER   63

green, yellow, and red stretched above the road ahead.
A lone balloon drifted up into the sky. Suddenly I understood why so many people were headed in one direction
and why the prevailing mood was so light. There must
be some kind of concert or festival going on. That meant
lots of people. Perfect for getting lost.

It turned out that the "festival" was just an evening
concert in another rather small park. It wasn't exactly
packed with people, as I had hoped, but at least the concert had drawn a decent crowd. Dozens of people lay
about on the grass, sleeping, picnicking, and soaking up
the festive mood. Others danced to the music close to
where the band was playing. At the far end of the park,
two tall, carved totem poles framed a spectacular view of
the sound.

I turned and scanned the streets behind me. Still
no sign of the mysterious blond-haired man. I wanted
to believe that I had ditched him, but that seemed too
easy. More likely, he was hiding somewhere. Watching.
A sense of dread rose up like a glacier wave, threatening
to crash down on my head.

I turned in a circle, suddenly feeling very alone in the
midst of all those people.

And then it began to register that the area I was in
had a familiar feel to it. I looked back toward the sound. I
could see the rise of the freeway, just beyond the edge of
the hill. The parking area where we left the car was down
there, which meant . . . I stepped up onto a low retaining

wall and looked down the street. With a rush of relief, I recognized the vendor stalls on the street in front of Pike Place Market.

I jumped down onto the sidewalk and ran for the Market. I could lose myself much better in the larger crowd there. And once I knew for sure I wasn't being followed, I could find my way to the parking lot. For the first time that entire day, I actually felt optimistic.

My optimism crumbled just a little as I neared the market. Instead of the crowd I had hoped for, just a handful of shoppers and tourists lingered. Most of the stalls were closed and a lot of the merchants were already disassembling them and sweeping the bricks around them. The long shadows that stretched between the buildings gave the scene a forlorn air.

Head low and radar high, I wandered past the remaining stalls, peering into storefronts and alleyways, behind booths, and down the shadowed street. And then I stumbled to a stop.

I blinked and rubbed my eyes. Just ahead, near a red-and-gold popcorn cart . . . I must've been seeing things, and yet there he stood. Instead of board shorts and sandals, he wore jeans and a T-shirt. He turned his head and his dark glasses caught the last rays of the sun. I couldn't breathe.

Seth.

Bit by bit, everything else faded away, like in one of

those old movies where all the action stops and the camera focuses in on just one person. All I could do was stare at him. It had only been weeks, but already my memory of him paled in comparison with the real thing. I hadn't forgotten the sharp curve of his jaw or the way his dark hair fell around his face, but I was delighted all over again by the way my stomach went all bubbly just from seeing him.

I called out his name, but I don't think he heard me. My first impulse was to run to him, but I thought better of it. What if I was still being followed? The last thing I wanted to do was drag Seth into whatever was going on.

It wasn't easy, but I let him walk right past me and managed not to reach out to touch him. He had stopped once again, and scanned the remaining booths like he was looking for something. Or someone. Had he come to the Market to find my mom and Joe? Was *he* the contact Joe had spoken of? I was still in such shock from seeing him that I didn't even wonder why he was in Seattle or how he had gotten there. That would come later. All that mattered at that moment was figuring out how I was going to alert Seth without drawing attention to him.

I followed him through the Market at a distance, watching him but being careful not to fully look in his direction. The way he strolled from one booth to the next, you'd think he was just any other tourist. I didn't miss the tension in his shoulders, though, or how his hands dug deep into his pockets the way they did whenever he was nervous or upset.

Finally, he moved from the outside stalls toward the arcade. If I was going to catch him, that would be the place to do it, before anyone looking on from outside could catch up to us. I quickened my pace, sidestepping merchants and their carts and managing to reach the entrance to the building about the same time as Seth.

I gripped his arm just long enough to get his attention and then walked ahead of him, hoping he would get the message and follow me. He did. I felt him at my elbow as I rushed toward the stairs that led to the lower-level shops. His footsteps echoed close behind mine.

The hallway below was deserted. The "DownUnder" shops apparently closed earlier than the booths on the arcade level. Still, I didn't like the idea of standing out in the open, just in case. I paused at the bottom of the stairs, looking for somewhere secluded that we could talk. The place was disappointingly lacking in hideaway nooks. Seth took the lead then, grabbing my hand without a word and pulling me down the hall until we reached an empty side hallway with a bolted door at the end of it.

He turned to face me and I couldn't help myself; I literally jumped at him and threw my arms around his neck. He didn't return the hug. I pulled away, embarrassed and confused.

"Seth," I said in a small voice, "what is it?"

He wouldn't meet my eyes, but looked down the hall. "I'm glad I found you," he said without feeling. "You know that ring I gave you at the resort? I need it back." His voice was cold. Detached.

Was he kidding? I stared at him. "That's it? You're not even going to say hello?"

"I'm serious."

And he was, too. I could tell by the hardness of his face. The icy glint to his blue eyes. My heart fell. "I . . . don't understand."

Seth dug his hands into his pockets again. "It's simple. I. Need. The. Ring."

My head spun. First my mom and then Seth. How could this be happening? My hand instinctively went to the spot on my chest where the ring usually rested. It wasn't there. I'm sure my panic must have shown on my face because his frown deepened.

"What is it? What's wrong?"

"It's gone! I always wear it on a chain. Right here." I splayed my hand over my chest. "I never take it off." Then my eyes grew wide as I remembered. "Except . . ."

"Except what?" I didn't like the urgency in Seth's voice.

"Except when I shower. I put it in my backpack this afternoon and—"

"Where is it now?"

"The ring or the backpack?"

He clenched his jaw. "Both."

I groaned as I remembered. My backpack was locked in the car. The car was in the parking lot. Where my mom might be waiting. I stepped back. "We need to go."

Seth grabbed my arm. His nostrils flared as he took a deliberate, deep breath. "*I* need the ring."

I shook him off. "Look, you can't just waltz in here and start making demands. I don't know what you're doing here, or how you got here or—"

He blew out a breath. "It doesn't matter."

My eyes stung and I blinked hard so that I wouldn't cry in front of him. "It *does* matter! I thought I'd never see you again, and here you show up with no hello and no explanation and the only thing you can say is give you back your ring? How can you be so obtuse? You have no idea what this day has been like. I just saw a man die, Seth. I don't even know if my mom is all right . . ." The words trailed off as my throat grew too tight to talk.

Seth's face softened—genuine sorrow flickering in his eyes—but just as quickly, they went blank again. "Look, I'm sorry for whatever you've been through, Aphra, and my week's been hell, too. The thing is, that ring belongs to my dad. I should never have given it to you."

"Oh." I stared at my feet. Maybe he was trying to make it easier, but it wasn't working. On the island, Seth told me that his dad had given him the ring when he was young. Seth had worn it for years. Maybe his dad got upset when he found out Seth had given the ring away, but I doubted it. Not upset enough to send him all the way to Seattle to retrieve it, anyway. Besides, something else was bothering Seth. I could feel it. "Why did you really come here?"

"To find you . . ." he said. I looked up, hopeful, until he continued ". . . so I could get the ring back."

"Oh."

"Where is it?"

I told him quickly how I had left the ring in my backpack, how I had locked the backpack in my mom's car, and all the events that had transpired since. Even though he managed to keep his expression blasé and impassive, his eyes told another story. They looked genuinely sad about Joe's death, but hardened again when I mentioned the man who had been following me.

"Where is he now?"

"I don't know." I glanced back toward the main hallway. "I lost sight of him just before I reached the Market."

"Do you know where the car is from here?"

"Yes." At least I hoped I did.

Seth followed me back up the stairs to the main level. By that time, most of the booths on the arcade level were either closed or shutting down. A few people still clustered around the restaurants and the remaining produce stalls, but other than that, the hall was clearing out.

I noticed with a pang that the stall Mom and Joe had occupied that morning was still set up with all of their pottery. A knot rose painfully in my throat and I swallowed hard against it. "This way," I managed to choke out. I pointed to the wide arcade doors.

We hadn't taken more than two steps before I saw a familiar blond head among the stragglers outside. My stalker stood on the cobbled street, casually scanning the crowd—for my face, I realized.

I grabbed Seth's arm to stop him and drew back behind the frame of an empty booth. The blond turned his head and an icy fist closed over my heart.

He was no random bad guy. He was a nightmare who had been haunting my dreams ever since he came to our island.

CHAPTER
5

I stood like a deer in the woods, afraid to move for fear it would attract a hunter's attention. Not that I could have moved if I'd wanted to. For several long, dreadful seconds, I was literally frozen in place. I couldn't even make myself speak, though I knew I should warn Seth.

All I could do was stare. How could it be? And yet there he was. The blond hair was new, but there was no mistaking the cold, dead eyes. The man outside was none other than Agent Watts of the CIA. But what was he doing there? Before my mind even formed the question, I knew the answer.

Earlier that summer, Watts had come to our island, chasing Seth and his family. I had no doubt that he was after Seth still . . . and I had led him right to his quarry. My head spun and fear roared in my ears. The whole day was like a bad dream that kept getting worse and worse.

As I looked at his predatory stance outside, it was hard to imagine that Watts had once been my mom's partner. Especially since their partnership had not engendered any loyalty as far as he was concerned. Where Mom had given up everything to protect the Mulos, Watts made it his mission to hunt them down. That I had stood in his way on the island had not helped matters. In fact, I'd made myself his sworn enemy when the herbs I had given him to make him sleep had some unpleasant side effects. He swore I had tried to poison him. At that moment I almost wished I had.

Seth's hand closed around my elbow and he leaned close. "What is it?"

His touch released me from my trance, but still I didn't move. "Watts," I whispered.

Seth didn't move, either, but his fingers tightened their grip, digging into my skin. "Where?"

I signaled with my eyes and Seth followed my gaze. At the same moment Watts raised his dull shark eyes and looked directly at us. His lips pulled back in what I swear was a snarl.

Seth spun and dragged me with him. We raced back to the stairs, bounding down two at a time. He grabbed my hand when we reached the lower level and drew me past the warren of shops behind the stairwell. We rattled on each door we passed, checking to see if any was open. I didn't expect any to be, so I was surprised when one metal door gave way. It led to what looked like a maintenance room, ladders, extension cords, and tools lining one wall and a control panel glowing with green and yellow lights on another. Seth herded me inside, closed the door behind us, and clicked the lock into place.

Except for the lights on the panel, it was pitch-black in

the room. I could barely make out the silhouette of Seth's head as he leaned close to me. "Where did you park?" he whispered.

"What?"

"The car! Where is it?"

I shook my head. "I don't know! I'm all turned around. We walked to it from the front of the Market this morning."

"Is it on a side street?"

"No. It was in a lot. Underneath the freeway."

"Close to the Market?"

"Yes. Just a couple blocks away. Down a steep hill. But I—"

Seth pressed his fingers to my lips. "Shhh!"

I heard it then, footsteps in the hallway outside. I groped for Seth's hand in the darkness and clung on to him, holding my breath. The footsteps drew nearer, slowed, and then stopped outside the door. I tensed, every muscle in my body coiled tight, ready to run. If only I had somewhere to run *to*.

The handle jiggled. The door rattled. I practically crushed Seth's hand.

And then the footsteps moved on. Still, I didn't dare move. Not for several minutes.

Finally, Seth whispered, "I think he's gone."

I realized I still had a death grip on his hand, so I slackened my grasp. I admit I had hoped he would hold

on to mine, but he didn't. I swallowed my disappointment and let my hand fall to my side.

"There are stairs at the other end of the hall," I offered.
"I saw them by the fish throwers' stall. If we can make
it down there, and then out to the front of the arcade, I
can find—"

"I think we can get to the parking lot from this level,"
Seth cut in. "There's a skywalk that leads straight there."

"Oh. How did you—"

"Last time I was here, your mom parked under the
freeway. She took us across a walkway to get there."

"Where is the walkway?"

"I *think* it's down to our right."

"But you're not sure."

"Only one way to find out." Slowly, carefully, he
opened the door. He checked the hallway and motioned
for me to follow him.

Back out in the corridor, I felt exposed, a moving target. At any moment Watts could return. I didn't want to
be around when he did.

A door at the end of the hall stood partway open, leading outside. We pushed through it and spilled out onto
a wooden deck overlooking the street below and the
sound beyond. From there, a covered walkway spanned
from the Market to a bank of elevators across the street.

"Bingo," Seth said.

We ran across the walkway and crowded into the

elevator along with half a dozen closing-time shoppers loaded with parcels and oversize bags. My stomach churned as the doors slid shut and we rode downward. For all we knew, Watts could be waiting for us below.

I was such a wreck by the time we reached the lower level that I had to bite my tongue to keep from crying out when the door slid open. Fortunately, there was no sign of Watts as we stepped out into the parking lot. Still, I didn't believe we were home free. The shadows provided too many places to hide. He could be anywhere.

"Where's the car?" Seth asked.

I pointed to the far end of the lot. "There. Near the street."

Cautiously, we wove past cars and trucks, vans and motorcycles. We had almost reached the spot where my mom and I had parked when she burst out from between two parked cars. "Aphra! Where have you—" Her eyes grew wide when she saw who was with me. "Seth?"

"Hello, Mrs. Connolly."

Her voice dropped to a low whisper. "How did you get here?" Her eyes slid right and then left. "What are you doing out in the open?"

"Mom, I saw—"

She shushed me and unlocked the car with a beep of her remote. "Not now. Get in!" Grabbing my shoulder, she practically shoved me into the backseat. Seth scrambled in after me.

I started to reach up into the front seat to grab my

backpack when she opened the driver's door. "Aphra, stay where you are." Her voice sounded unnaturally calm. She slid into her seat and stabbed the keys into the ignition. "Both of you stay low and quiet until I tell you otherwise, understand?"

I dropped onto the seat and ducked down so that I couldn't see out—or be seen through—the window. Seth crouched next to me, draping an arm over my back. At first I was touched by his protectiveness, but as soon as we got out on the road, I could see he was just being practical. Hunched over as we were, it was hard to keep our balance. Whenever we went around a corner, we had to brace ourselves to keep from tipping over. I didn't really mind the turns, though, because when centripetal force pushed us together and I was pressed against him even for a moment, I felt safe.

Mom drove for several miles before she spoke, her voice tight and sharp. "How could you be so predictable, Seth? We've been monitoring the chatter at the Agency since you left the island, and you know what they say? Watch the girl and you'll find the boy. And you proved them right!" She shook her head, glaring at us through the rearview mirror. "I really thought you were smarter than this. The protocol exists to protect you."

"I understand. But . . . I didn't have a choice. Aphra has something of mine."

"What could possibly be important enough to risk the lives of everyone in this operation?"

His voice cracked. "A ring."

Mom strangled the steering wheel. "Explain."

"I . . . gave it to Aphra. My dad needs it."

Mom growled and yanked the car sharply to the left. I fell against Seth, but this time I didn't find any comfort in the contact. The hum of the tires sounded different, like the road's surface had changed. Sure enough, Mom slowed and the ride got bumpier. Finally, she swung the car in a wide arc, threw it into park, and killed the engine.

Trees loomed overhead and the sharp smell of pine filled the air. It looked like we were in some kind of nature park, with cedar-chip trails that led off into the shadowed wood.

Mom twisted around in her seat. "Aphra, where is Seth's ring?"

"It's in my backpack."

She hefted the pack and threw it over the seat back. It landed with a thud beside me. "Give it to him. And then, Seth, you are going to tell me what this is all about."

I sat up and zipped open the outside pouch. I felt inside. My stomach dropped. The pouch was empty.

Seth must have read the look on my face because he grabbed my backpack from me and shoved his hand inside the pouch. Finding it empty, he unzipped the bigger pouch and yanked out my toothbrush and toothpaste. My hairbrush dropped to the floor.

I tried to pull the pack away from him. "It was in the top one. That's the only place I ever put it."

He swatted away my hand and continued his search, dumping out my clothes and pawing through them.

I grabbed a wayward bra and stuffed it back into the pack. "Stop it! I said it wasn't there!"

"It has to be." He sifted through my things again. The desperation in his face scared me.

"Seth, what's going on?"

But he didn't answer. Instead, he wrenched open the door and bolted out of the car. I jumped out my side and raced after him. Mom ran after both of us.

Seth stomped back and forth, fists clenched so hard that the veins stood out on his arms. He kicked the wooden park bench that sat at the mouth of one trail and spun to face me. His face was livid and his eyes blue ice. "How could you lose that ring?"

I swallowed drily. I had never seen Seth angry before. It scared me. "I didn't lose it," I said weakly.

"Then where is it?"

"I don't know! Like I told you, I put it in my backpack when I took a shower this morning. I always put it right back on, but Joe pushed me out of the bathroom and—" A cold realization swept over me. "Joe! He must have taken it from my backpack."

"Why would he do that?" Seth's voice was approaching hysterical. "How would he even know it was there?"

Mom's voice was quiet. "He was searching her bag."

"He what?"

She bristled. "It was his job. Whenever we processed

people, he would go through their things. We had to be certain where their loyalties lay."

I stared at her. Great. My own mom didn't trust me.

"Don't give me that look, Aphra. I didn't authorize him to go through *your* bag."

"Authorize?" I asked. "Was he your subordinate, then?"

She rubbed a hand over her face. Suddenly she looked very tired. "He *was* my partner."

It sounded so plaintive, the way that she said that, and I wasn't sure if it was because Joe was gone, or because she suspected Stuart was right and Joe had been contacting the Agency behind her back.

"Did Joe say anything about the ring when he called you?" I asked.

"Not specifically. He did say there was something I needed to see and I had to meet him right away. But then..."

Seth sat heavily on the bench. "Someone got to him first."

"Suppose you tell me what's so important about this ring," Mom said. "Then maybe we can figure out why Joe would have wanted to take it."

Seth rolled his lips inward. "I can't."

"Seth, it's me! I've been with your family for years. If there's something wrong, I need to know about it."

He just glared at her. "You split us up. I didn't even know my dad wouldn't be meeting us until Mom and I got to Sydney."

She sighed. "We needed to make you harder to track. Splitting you up was the best option we had."

"Well, it didn't work. They found him."

Mom's mouth went slack. "When?"

"Couple of days ago. They want the ring, Natalie. If I don't get it for them within five days . . ."

The ground felt like it was tilting sideways. Last time I had seen Seth, we'd come face-to-face with an assassin who had been sent to silence Seth's family. Her black eyes and wicked smile still haunted my dreams. I could hardly breathe, remembering how she had tried to kill Seth and me. But the authorities had taken her into custody. Had she escaped? "Who has your dad, Seth?"

He didn't even look up. "I don't know. The Mole wants him dead. The CIA thinks he's a liability."

Mom's face tightened. From what she had told me, I knew what she must be thinking: the CIA didn't think he was a liability; the Mole's minions *within* the CIA thought he was a liability. Either way, something about the scenario the way Seth explained it didn't make sense.

"You said they're holding him," I said to Seth, "but if they want him dead, why didn't they just kill him when they found him?"

His head whipped up and I could have hit myself for causing the panic and grief I saw in his eyes.

"I . . . I'm sorry. That didn't come out right." I sat beside him and tried to take his hand, but he moved it away. I bit my lip and looked up to my mom for help.

"What Aphra was trying to ask—rather indelicately—was why the change in tactics? What makes them so interested in this ring that they would create a hostage situation to get it?"

A shadow passed over Seth's face. It was subtle, but it was there. He took a breath like he was going to say something and then he clamped his mouth shut. "I . . . I don't know why they want it," he said finally. "Dad never told me it was special. Not like that, anyway. I thought it was just an old class ring or something. I would never have given it away if I'd known . . ."

I felt like the biggest scum that had ever walked the earth. How could I lose the one thing Seth had entrusted me with? "Mom, think. Where could Joe have put it if he took it?"

She shook her head helplessly. "I wish I knew. Stuart's been monitoring the Agency daily and nothing has been said about a ring. None of this makes sense."

I agreed. "It *doesn't* make sense. If they—whoever they are—knew where Seth and his mom were, why wouldn't they just go after them? If Mr. Mulo told them Seth had the ring—"

"He never told them that I had it," Seth cut in. "They think my mom—"

"Whatever. My point is, if they knew where you were, why wouldn't they just come get it?"

"They didn't necessarily know where we were, even with the phone call. My mom and dad had international cell phones so they could keep in touch, and they never stayed on long enough for tracking."

Mom frowned. "Cell phones were not part of the plan."

"I guess they made it part of the plan."

"Are you sure they really have your dad?" I asked. "What if they're using this ring thing just to flush you out?"

Seth looked to the ground. His voice dropped to barely a whisper. "They . . . cut off his finger while they were on the phone. My mom heard him scream."

My stomach heaved and darkness crowded around the corners of my vision. I thought I was going to lose it right there, but I had to be strong . . . for Seth. At least that's what I told myself.

"I need the ring," Seth said firmly, "to keep my dad alive."

"Mom?" My throat was so tight I could hardly force out the words. "Where is Joe's body? What if he had the ring with him?"

"He didn't. I managed to gather all his personal effects before the paramedics arrived." Her voice grew even more distant. "It's protocol. There was no ring."

"Where could he have put it?"

"I don't know," she said. "If he didn't have it with him this morning, it must still be at the apartment."

Seth jumped to his feet. "Then what are we doing here? We have to go find it!"

• • •

None of us spoke as we drove back to the apartment building. There was nothing to say. We had to find the ring. Beyond that . . . I didn't want to think about it.

The first thing I noticed when we pulled into the garage was Stuart, wiping down the handles of the van. He must have driven it home earlier from the Market parking lot. I assumed he was wiping it clean of fingerprints. His or Joe's, I didn't know.

He rushed the car when he saw it was us. "Nat! Where have you *been*? I was about ready to clear out. I thought you might have—" His words died when his gaze slid to the backseat and he saw Seth. "Mulo?"

Seth dipped his head in greeting.

For the first time since I'd met him, Stuart seemed to be at a loss for words. He just stood there, staring at Seth. "When . . . ? How . . . ?"

Mom climbed from the car and filled Stuart in as much as she could. He listened silently, though I could see the agitation building as his face grew redder and the little muscle at the corner of his jaw tightened and twitched.

He removed his glasses and pinched the bridge of his nose. "So Aphra had this ring all along," he finally said when Mom was through.

I nodded. "Until this morning."

"We need to look for it," Seth put in.

"Here? Now?" Stuart was incredulous. "We don't have

time. We should already be gone as it is. As soon as the police identify Joe—"

"Joe has no identity," Mom cut in flatly. "He never existed."

"Right." Stuart crossed his arms. "Tell that to the people who saw him expire this morning. Tell it to the paramedics who—"

"Who will not know who he is."

"Our cover is blown, Natalie. People at the Market have seen you and Joe together for months. How long do you think it will be before they start asking questions?"

"We'll be quick," she said.

Stuart folded his arms and muttered, "This is not wise." Still, he followed us inside.

In a cluster, we clamored up the stairs and burst into the apartment. Mom led the way to Joe's small room. Right away I could tell it wouldn't be a simple search. Unlike Stuart, neatness was obviously not Joe's thing. A blanket lay in a puddle next to his bed. The pillow had fallen back against the wall. Papers littered the floor and clothes were scattered everywhere—on the bed, on the floor, draped over the lone chair, and tumbling out of an army duffel.

Among the four of us, we scoured every inch of that room. Twice. Seth even checked all the floorboards to make sure there were no hidey-holes anywhere. No luck.

"We'll search the entire apartment if we have to,"

Mom assured him. "If Joe took that ring, it has to be around somewhere."

I chewed the inside of my cheek, wondering why my mom would say such a thing. My gut told me she was wrong, and I had to believe she knew it, too. Joe left that morning shortly after he came out of the bathroom. That didn't really give him much time to hide anything in the apartment. And just because Mom didn't find the ring when she went through his "personal effects" at the coffee shop didn't mean he hadn't taken it with him. He could have hidden it anywhere along the way. Plus, he'd been gone for a good long while before he called to tell Mom where he would be. She had to wonder what he'd been doing all that time. On the other hand, none of this changed anything. Of course we had to look. Before we cleared out, we had to be certain the ring had not been left in the apartment.

Mom began handing out orders like a drill sergeant. "Aphra, check the bathroom; Seth, start going through the cupboards and drawers in the kitchen; I'll search the den; and Stuart, you take the front room."

I had to give Stuart credit; he set to work without question, flipping over his carefully positioned couch cushions. And even though he was the one who was antsy for us to clear out of the apartment, he pulled out all the stops searching the place. He even dug his hands through the soil of the potted plants. It didn't improve his mood, though. By the time we had finished searching the apartment, the stairwell, and the garage, day had turned to night outside. With each passing moment, Stuart was becoming more and more irritable.

"This is not protocol. We should have been gone a long time ago."

Mom shrugged him off. "It's better to leave after dark, anyway," she told him. He just tightened his lips and finished packing up his computers.

Seth was inconsolable. He paced in the corner, muttering, "What am I going to do?"

I tried to comfort him, but he just glared at me. "You're the one who lost the ring."

"I didn't lose it! It was taken from me."

"It wouldn't have been taken if you hadn't left it."

"I did *not* leave it!"

He folded his arms and turned away.

Mom was gathering her papers and arguing with Stuart. When she caught me watching, her face turned cold, almost hostile. I couldn't take it anymore. I had to get away from Mom, from Stuart, and especially from Seth.

No one even noticed when I slipped out the door and into the hallway. I wanted to scream. To punch something. To punch myself.

I never thought I'd say it, but I wanted to go home. If I were back on the island, I could pretend the whole trip never happened. I could pretend my mom wanted me to find her. I could pretend Seth liked me. I could pretend I didn't feel like the biggest loser on the face of the earth.

But pretending never made anything true. In reality I knew I could never go back. Not to the way things were. Too much had happened. I pushed through the door to the stairwell and ran blindly down the steps, not stopping until I spilled out into the garage. The lights flicked on—thanks to the stupid sensor over the door. I hugged my arms and sank down along the edge of the wall, waiting for them to click off again. It was hard enough to face the reality of the cold, stark garage, the overpowering smell of rubber, grease, and motor oil, and the fact that I had let a lot of people down. I didn't need the glare of the light highlighting my flaws.

A tear rolled down my cheek and I swiped it away. I had no right feeling sorry for myself when Mom had lost a partner and Seth's dad was being held hostage somewhere.

The lights had barely turned off when the door opened and they blazed on again. Seth's broad shoulders filled the doorway, but there was a posture of defeat to them, and in the hesitant way that he stepped through the opening. I turned my face away from him, scrubbing my hands over my eyes to hide the tears. The last thing I wanted was for him to see me crying.

The click of the heavy metal door closing echoed through the garage and I could hear Seth's footsteps on the rough concrete floor. "Aphra?" His voice sounded as if it had lost its edge, but I'd lost all faith in my ability to guess what he might be thinking. I didn't answer.

He took another step. "Aphra, I'm sorry. I didn't mean to blame you."

"But it's my fault." My voice sounded small. Pitiful.

He closed the distance between us and touched a tentative hand to my shoulder. "It's getting cold. I grabbed this from the apartment for you."

I looked up to see him holding out a Seahawks sweatshirt. His gesture made me feel even worse. I stood and took the sweatshirt from him, unable to look in his face. I dutifully slipped it on over my head and stood awkwardly, struggling for something to say.

"I'm so sorry, Seth." My voice cracked.

"You didn't know."

"What you must be going through . . ."

He dug his hands into the pockets of his jeans and hunched his shoulders. "They hurt my dad," he said. He sounded lost and frightened.

Tears filled my eyes once more, but I was no longer ashamed of them. They were for Seth, not for me. "I'm sorry," I whispered again. He held my gaze for a long while and then brushed a tear from my cheek with the back of his finger.

"Ah, jeez, Aphra." His voice was rough and husky. "I didn't mean to . . ." He took my hand hesitantly, almost shyly, and drew me to him. The garage lights flickered off and in the darkness I found the courage to wrap my arms around his waist. I laid my cheek against his chest, listening to the rhythm of his heart. He smelled like I remembered, felt like I remembered. I wanted to cry for real.

Because even though in that moment I finally had what I had wanted—to be with Seth, his arms around me—I realized with painful clarity that was not how it would always be. Seth and I would never end up together. We couldn't. If we stayed alive long enough to find the ring and save Seth's dad, the Mulos would have to run again. And if what my mom said was true, I would always act as a kind of divining rod that the bad guys could use to lead them to Seth. The only safe thing for us to do would be to stay apart.

I held him tighter, knowing that it might be the last time I ever would. We could have stood like that all night and I would have been happy. But I knew the clock was ticking. Mom and Stuart would be ready to clear out at any time. Whoever had killed Joe could be looking for us next. I had to set things right and then step out of Seth's life forever.

I pulled back, wiping my eyes. "We can't give up."

In the shadows, I couldn't read Seth's face. He didn't say anything, but his head moved. Maybe he was nodding in agreement. I didn't know.

With new determination, I pushed away and marched toward the door.

"What are you doing?"

"I'll find it for you, Seth. If I have to retrace Joe's steps from the moment he left the apartment, I'll find it."

"Don't be crazy. What are you going to do, walk to the city? Do you even know how to get there from here?"

"I'll . . . I'll take the car. I have a pretty good sense of direction. I can find the way."

He made an incredulous sound in his throat. "Right. You think your mom's going to just hand over her keys?"

"I wouldn't ask her."

"Aphra. Be real. Your mom and Stuart worked for the CIA. You're not going to be able to swipe anything without them knowing."

"Well, I can't just sit around and do nothing! It's making me crazy."

He stuffed his hands into his pockets again. "I know."

The pain in his voice deflated my bravado. I felt empty inside. Helpless. "Seth, I need you to know how sorry I am."

"I do know." His voice was gruff. "But it's my own fault. I didn't know the ring was such a big deal."

I edged closer until I could see the worry line his face as deeply as the shadows. "*Why* is it such a big deal, Seth? Why do they want it so much?"

He looked at me with an intensity I'd never seen in him before—like he wanted to tell me something, but he wasn't sure if he could.

I drew his hand from his pocket and clutched it in my own. "You can trust me, Seth."

He bobbed his head, but still didn't say anything for what felt like a very long time. Finally, he spoke in a low voice, barely a whisper. "The ring . . . contains a list."

"It *contains* a list? What kind of list? How?"

His hand slipped from mine. "I . . . can't say . . ."

That wasn't exactly the answer I was hoping for, but I knew better than to pursue it. Yet. "Seth, the people who are holding your dad . . . what do they want the ring for?"

"I don't know. I only heard one side of the phone call."

I swallowed, remembering what Seth had said about his mom having to hear his dad scream on the other end of the line. I couldn't even imagine the helplessness and horror she must have felt. "How is your mom dealing with all this?"

He shrugged and looked down at his feet.

"Why didn't she come with you?"

"She didn't know I was leaving."

"What?"

"I wasn't meant to hear the phone call. It came in the middle of the night. She probably thought I was asleep. All I could think was that it was my fault. I had given the ring away; I had to get it back."

I took his hand again. "We'll find it. If we have to—" I blinked. "Wait. A list! I almost forgot! Joe talked about a list, too. Right before he died."

Seth's eyes widened. "What? What did he say?"

"I'm not sure I remember it all. It didn't make sense to me at the time. Plus he didn't give me complete sentences, just random words. At least I thought they were random."

He tightened his fingers around mine. "Think, Aphra. What exactly did he say?"

I screwed my eyes shut tight, trying to remember. "Something about a list and a . . . a cup or something. I thought he was talking about his coffee cup. Like he knew he'd been poisoned. I watched him, Seth. I saw him take a drink and then he started jerking and fell to the ground and I ran to him and . . ." I tried to erase the image of his panicked face from my mind. "He could hardly take a breath."

"When did he tell you about the list?"

"He said 'the list is . . .'" I grasped at the air as if I could find the answer hanging there. "*In* something."

"In the cup?"

"Cup *holder*! That's what it was, a cup holder."

"What kind of cup holder? Like for takeout? What does that mean?"

"I don't know. He didn't have any cup holder with him."

"Are you sure he didn't say anything else?"

"I'm sure." I could barely stand under the weight of Seth's stare. It was like he was trying to *will* me into understanding exactly what Joe was talking about. But I didn't. Unless . . . "Wait. What if he was talking about the cup holder in the van? Maybe the ring is in there."

We raced to where the van was parked, but the door was locked. Seth cupped his hands around his eyes and peered through the window.

"Do you see anything?"

"No," he said. "It's too dark."

"We have to get the keys."

"Wait!"

I stopped midstep. "What? Why?"

"I don't want to alert Stuart and your mom." He glanced pointedly at the stairwell door. "If we find the ring, we don't say anything to them, okay?"

"I don't understand."

"We don't know who has my dad. I trust your mom, but . . ."

"But they're probably watching her."

"Right. And she said herself that there may be a leak in the Agency. It would be better for everyone if they think I'm going home empty-handed. At least until I can take care of my dad."

"Okay." I looked around the shadowed garage. "But how are we going to get into the van?"

"We need some wire."

We searched quickly among the shelves and castoffs scattered around the garage, but there was no wire to be found except for some flimsy, plastic-coated electric wire, and that wasn't what we wanted, according to Seth. "It needs to be sturdy enough to pull up the pin."

The words were familiar enough to me—I'd learned to pick household locks from our super back at the resort—but I couldn't envision the inside mechanics of a car door.

"Wait. I got it." Seth popped the arm off the windshield wiper. "It has a U-hook on the end. I can use that."

He slid the makeshift hook down between the window gasket and the window, fishing inside the door.

I folded my arms. "I don't even want to know where you learned to do this."

"I lived near Detroit," he said. Like that explained anything.

I glanced nervously at the stairwell. Any moment, Mom and Stuart could be ready to leave. I doubted either one of them would appreciate us messing with the van . . . or keeping whatever we discovered a secret. "Quickly!"

The lock clicked.

Seth climbed into the van and I pushed in behind him. We felt in the dark for the plastic cup holders. One of those insulated aluminum coffee cups sat in the hole closer to the driver's side. The little sipping spout was half open and I could smell the remains of Joe's coffee— bitter and black. I lifted it gingerly. It felt creepy handling his cup, but I had to check beneath it, just in case.

Nothing. The look on Seth's face told me he had found nothing in the other side, either. Another dead end.

I wasn't ready to give up yet. "What about . . . Could he have put the ring in the *car* before he went to the coffee shop?"

"Only one way to find out."

I jumped out of the van and ran to the car. Crossing my fingers, I grasped the handle. "It's open," I called softly.

I climbed into the car and felt for the cup holder. Unfortunately, this one slid out from the dash like a CD drive on a computer. It featured two holes cut into the molded plastic that cups could fit into. There was no room for a ring to be hidden behind the mechanism.

Seth peered in through the open door. "Well?"

"Nothing."

I could literally feel his disappointment, but what did he expect? It had been a dumb idea, anyway. If this ring was so valuable, there's no way Joe would have left it lying around in a cup holder where anyone could see it.

I froze. He *wouldn't* have wanted anyone to see it. He would have hidden it. "Back to the van! We've got to pull it out."

"What?"

"The cup holder. It's just molded plastic sunk in a hole in the console. He could have put the ring beneath it."

I didn't need to say anything more. We raced to the van and clawed at the edge of the cup holder until we were finally able to pry it up.

I felt around the vacant hole, checking for secret compartments or other covert stuff like that. Clearly the vehicles were standard issue, because there were no James Bond–type features anywhere.

Dejected, I fitted the cup-holder piece back into the hole. I grabbed the coffee cup from where it had fallen on the floor, dribbling coffee all over the floor mat. It rattled. I drew in a breath. A slosh I might expect, but a rattle?

I dumped the coffee out the door. It splattered on the garage floor.

"What are you doing?" Seth hissed.

"Hold on." Hands trembling, I unscrewed the lid and upended the cup. Out slid the ring, still attached to my chain.

"You got it," Seth breathed.

Just then, the lights flicked on. I blinked against the sudden glare and closed my fist around the ring.

"What's going on?" Mom marched across the garage, followed closely by Stuart. "What are you doing in there? Get out this instant."

Seth climbed out the passenger-side door and I climbed out the driver's side, slipping the ring into my pocket as I went.

"We were just searching the van," Seth explained.

"Well?" Stuart looked beyond me and into the van through the open door. "What did you find?"

I made my face go blank. "Nothing."

He pushed past me to see for himself and stepped right in the puddle of spilled coffee. He looked down.

I rushed to redirect his attention. "Um . . . what if he left it in the coffee shop? We should go back there and—"

"Absolutely not." The light danced on his glasses as he shook his head. "You don't think the police will have that place staked out?"

"But—"

"Too dangerous. Besides, I'm sure the Agency has scoured the place from top to bottom by now."

"Oh." I tried to look suitably disappointed as I shut the van door. "Just trying to help."

Stuart gave me a condescending pat on the arm. "And we appreciate it. We've really wasted enough time, Natalie. We need to move out now."

Mom gave a resigned sigh. "I am so sorry," she said to Seth. "We'll figure something out."

Seth hung his head like he was completely defeated. Even though I knew he was only acting, it broke my heart. "I understand," he managed.

Mom and Stuart headed back inside. At the door, Mom paused and turned back to us. "Be ready to leave in five."

I nodded, afraid to speak for fear I'd give something away. The moment she closed the door, Seth rushed to where I was standing.

"Where is it?" he whispered.

I pulled the chain from my pocket and held it out to him, the ring swinging like a pendulum.

He grabbed it and clutched it to his chest. "Yes!"

"So you still have time to help your dad, right?"

His smile faded. "I hope so."

"Can you call them? Tell them you're coming?"

"Not without tipping off everyone else."

"Who's everyone? Who else is after this ring, Seth?"

He wouldn't meet my eyes. "I don't know."

"I think you do. I also think you know *why* they're after it." It wasn't an accusation. Just a fact.

Finally, he looked at me. "The ring contains a very important list."

My stomach twisted. The list again. Is that why Joe was killed? "What kind of list are we talking about?"

"A list of names." Seth waited for that to sink in, and then added, "Sleepers."

I drew in a breath. The other members of his parents' sleeper cell! I thought of how I had been carrying that ring around for the last couple of months and my head felt light. But . . . I had never seen any lists. And it's not like there were a lot of hiding places in a ring. "How is that possible?"

"I'll show you." Seth held the ring up toward the light. "Look. The names are etched into the back of the stone."

I squinted at the ring, searching. "What? Those little scratches?"

"Yeah. You'd have to use a microscope or something to read it, but those little scratches could reveal the identity and alias of every sleeper agent in that organization."

"Wow."

"No kidding."

"Isn't your family's name on the—"

He held up his hand, signaling me to be quiet. "Did you hear that?"

I shook my head.

"Hold on." He handed me back the ring. "I thought I heard something." He crept toward the stairwell door and I followed close behind. We didn't find anything, but it was enough to shake us up.

I stuffed the ring into my pocket and took Seth's hand. "Wait for the lights to die," I whispered. "We'll head outside."

We stood next to the wall until the lights clicked off and then climbed up the ramp to the street, keeping close to the edge so that the sensors wouldn't pick up our movement and trip them on again. At street level, we had almost stepped into a puddle of light from the streetlamp when my attention was drawn to a car parked on the opposite side of the street. I wouldn't have noticed it had it not been for something glowing and red in the front seat of the car. It seemed to hover in the air, grow brighter red, then dull again. A cigarette. I pushed Seth deeper into the shadows. "Someone's in that car."

Sure enough, the red glowed bright one more time

before we heard the mechanical whir of the power window rolling down. The cigarette flipped from the car, drawing a red arc in the air. Seconds later, the stench of burning tobacco wafted toward us.

"What's he doing?" I whispered.

"You think someone's watching the apartment?"

"Could be."

Just then, the driver lit another cigarette, cupping his hand over the flame so that the glow illuminated his face. I sucked in a breath. Same blond hair, same cold eyes. I drew back against Seth.

"What is it?"

My blood ran cold just thinking about him.

"Watts."

CHAPTER
6

Seth swore. "What is Watts doing here?"

"What do you think?"

Grabbing my hand, Seth pulled me back into the garage. He drew me against him again, but not romantically this time. We were both terrified. At least I was terrified, and I figured Seth was, too, the way his heart was racing.

"We can't go out this way," he murmured.

"You think?"

He took my hand. "Come on. *This* we need to tell your mom and Stuart."

We felt our way back through the garage, not even worrying about the light this time. We ran up the stairs and burst into the apartment.

Stuart must have been right at the door when it flew open because he jumped back, swearing. "Watch it!"

"Watts is here," I blurted.

"What? Impossible."

"I saw him outside. He was—"

"You recognized him in the dark?"

"Yes!"

Stuart looked to Seth. "Did you see him?"

Seth nodded and Stuart's face grew serious. "Where?"

He turned and yelled over his shoulder, "Nat? We've got a problem."

Mom rushed over to where we were clustered near the door. "What is it?"

I told her how we had seen Watts sitting in the car in front of the apartment building.

"Was he alone?"

"I don't know. It was dark."

"I told you we should have cleared out long ago," Stuart muttered.

"Well, we're clearing out now. Out back toward the locks. Let's go."

"Where are we going to go?" I asked.

"To the lake. We have a boat."

"What? You never said anything about a boat before."

She shook her head. "There was no need. We only share what information is necessary."

How could I ask anything else after she said that? Maybe I didn't need more answers, anyway. If I thought about it, pieces began to fall into place on their own. I had assumed that the reason they had moved into that particular apartment building was simply that the apartment owner was gone on sabbatical, but they had purposely chosen a place on the waterfront.

It made sense that they would have a boat nearby, and an alternative escape route. According to Ryan, the locks connected Lake Union with the sound and eventually the ocean. This way, they weren't landlocked.

Mom led us down the slope to a path that wound along the locks to the lake. As we neared the first dock, she instructed us to slow down. "Act natural," she said.

Seth threw me a pained look and I raised my shoulders. So it was cliché. It also happened to be smart.

"Aphra? Hey, Aphra. Is that you?"

I jumped and turned around.

Ryan strode out of the shadows carrying a duffel bag. Sweat glistened along his hairline and he was breathing heavily, like he'd been running. "What a pleasant surprise to see you here. How's it going?"

I forced a smile. "Good. And you?"

"Good." His eyes strayed to Seth, then to Mom and Stuart in turn.

"So," I said, directing his attention back to me. "What are you up to tonight?"

"Heading out." He lifted the bag in evidence. "Game's over."

"Oh. Right. Who won?"

"Mariners by a run."

"Sounds like a good game."

"It was."

I could practically feel Mom's eyes boring into my back. I shifted uncomfortably. She would be wondering how I knew Ryan, and the answer wouldn't sound good. I snuck out of the apartment—not once but twice—discussed personal information with a stranger, and by so doing had compromised our clean escape. I had to get rid of Ryan without making it seem like that's what I was trying to do, since it might draw more attention to our presence on the docks.

I glanced up at the sky, where a handful of dark clouds blotted out the moon. "I better not keep you. It looks like rain."

"Naw, that's nothing."

"Well, *we* should get going," Mom cut in pleasantly. "Nice to meet you, Mister . . . ?"

"Anderson, ma'am. Ryan Anderson." He shifted his duffel to his left hand and extended his right. "I believe we're neighbors."

Mom's brows raised ever so slightly, but she maintained her smile. "Well, then. Perhaps we'll see you around."

"Yes, ma'am. Good night."

Ryan dipped his head in farewell and walked off down the path, gravel crunching beneath his feet.

I didn't want to look in my mom's face. Or Stuart's, or Seth's for that matter. I stared at the ground.

"Let's go," she said, voice grating.

We clomped down the dock to the last pier, where the boat—a small open utility boat with an outboard motor—was tied. Mom started undoing the moorings while Stuart reached down to start the motor.

Hot white light flashed. The air felt like it was being sucked from my lungs, and my head rang as if someone had clapped their hands over my ears. Hard. I don't remember falling, but the next thing I knew, I was sitting on the dock, head pounding. The boat was a mass of flames. Papers fluttered down all around us. It didn't—couldn't—register for a full second what had happened. I think I tried to scream, but my voice had lost its power. Mom lay crumpled around a pier like a broken doll. It probably saved her from being thrown into the water. I crawled over to her on my hands and knees.

"Mom! Mom!" She didn't respond. I twisted about in a panic, looking for Stuart. He'd know what to do. But Stuart was writhing on the deck, clutching his hand to his chest. Seth sat not far from where we were, shaking his head and looking dazed.

"Seth, are you all right?"

He nodded slowly, as if he wasn't quite sure.

"See if you can help Stuart!"

Seth swayed to his feet and stumbled over to where Stuart lay and I turned my attention back to my mom.

I felt along her neck for a pulse. I couldn't tell if the pounding I felt in my fingers was my own pulse or hers. "Mom! Can you hear me?"

She moaned and her head lolled to the side. I almost cried. At least she was alive. I checked her over quickly, looking for injuries. Even in the darkness, her face looked red, as if she were badly sunburned. Other than that, she seemed fine. No blood, no broken bones. The impact of the explosion could have knocked her out. Either from that, or slamming into the pier. The important thing was that she appeared to be otherwise unharmed.

I wished I could say the same for Stuart. Once I had made sure my mom was okay, I turned to help Seth. What I saw horrified me. Stuart's glasses tilted on his head, the right lens shattered. His face was black from the flash and he still cradled his left hand to his chest. His shirt was soaked in blood. Blackened, bloody stubs were all that was left of his ring and pinkie fingers.

My stomach heaved and I looked quickly away. I wanted to cry, but that wouldn't do us any good. The explosion may have alerted Watts. We had to get out of there. And then we had to get Stuart medical attention.

"Aphra! What happened?" Ryan ran down the dock toward us. "I saw the flash. It sounded like an explosion."

But before I could answer, headlights swung over the lip of the road back by the path. Watts's car. There was no time for explanations.

"Ryan! We need your help!" I jumped to my feet and grabbed his hand. "That guy is after us." He followed my gaze to where Watts—in a suit and tie now—jumped out of the car. "We need to get out of here!"

He hesitated for a second, but when he saw Mom lying on the pier and Stuart's injuries, he nodded gravely.

"The plane," he yelled. "I'm on the next dock over and already prepped to take off. Come on!"

He scooped my mom up from the dock like it was no

effort at all. "Help them," he yelled, nodding to where Seth was trying to pull Stuart to his feet. "Let's go!"

I grabbed Stuart's good hand and slung his arm over my shoulder. Seth propped him up from the other side. I tried not to look at Stuart's mangled hand or the blood or his wide-eyed stare. "It's going to be okay," I assured him. "We're going to get you out of here."

We had to practically drag Stuart to where Ryan's plane bobbed gently in the water. The whole time I felt like a huge, lumbering target. I glanced back to see Watts running down the hill toward the path. "He's coming!"

Ryan set my mom on her feet and motioned for me to hold her. Seth grabbed Stuart so that he wouldn't fall over and I rushed to hold up my mom. She leaned heavily against me, moaning. At least she was coming to. Ryan clamored onto the landing skids and threw open the latch on the door. "Get in!"

I handed my mom back to him and climbed through the door. He passed her to me and I pulled her inside, propping her against the wall of the plane. When I poked my head back out the door, I saw that Watts had reached the path.

"Hurry! Hurry!"

Seth pushed Stuart forward, but Stuart twisted and strained in his arms.

"No," he growled. "No!"

"Get in!" Ryan ordered.

"Nooooo."

Seth wrestled Stuart onto the skid where Ryan was waiting to hand him up into the plane. Stuart must have been crazy with pain, the way he kept screaming and resisting, but among the three of us, we got him inside.

Ryan scrambled in after him and clanged the door shut behind him. He bolted up to the front, slid into one of the only two seats on the plane, and started throwing switches. The plane shuddered and vibrated as the engines roared to life and the propellers kicked in.

"Hold on!" Ryan yelled as the plane began to glide forward.

Hold on to what? We were crammed into an empty freight area, with nothing but a couple of cargo nets stretched floor to ceiling and a hand truck strapped to the wall. No jump seats. And more importantly, no seat belts.

I grabbed the securing straps for the cargo nets and tethered my mom and myself to the wall. Seth tried to do the same with Stuart, but Stuart kept swatting him away. Somewhere along the way he'd lost his glasses and he squinted fiercely, growling obscenities. Finally, Seth gave up and wrapped a strap around himself. Stuart curled into a ball in the corner, hand tucked up under his armpit.

Unsteadily, the plane jumped and skipped like a drunken albatross, wings dipping left then right before steadying and tilting upward, pulling us up into the air.

My ears popped as we climbed and my head still rang, but we'd made it. We were alive and together. That was all that mattered.

The plane steadied once we leveled off. I undid the straps and took a long look at Stuart. I was afraid he might go into shock—or that he already had. He seemed confused and disoriented and that wasn't a good sign.

"Ryan! Do you have a first-aid kit?"

He didn't answer. Probably couldn't hear me above the roar of the plane. I crawled to the back of his chair and saw that he was wearing headphones. I gestured at him to remove them. "Do you have a first-aid kit?" I yelled.

"In the corner!" He waved vaguely behind him. The plane wiggled when he took his hand off the controls and he quickly straightened it.

My stomach flipped and I fought a sudden wave of motion sickness. I'd never experienced it before, but our resort manager Darlene got motion sick nearly every time she climbed into our helicopter on the island. It didn't even have to be off the ground for her to start turning green. She always wore special motion-sickness bracelets to help her cope. I used to laugh at her for it, but now I struggled to remember what pressure points those bracelets hit because I really didn't have time to get sick. I slid to the floor of the plane, leaning up against the back of the chair as I felt along my wrist with two fingers, like a nurse taking a pulse.

Seth crawled over beside me.

"Are you okay?" he yelled.

"I'll be fine. Just a little sick to my stomach." I worked up a shaky smile. "Stay with my mom, will you? I'm going to try to help Stuart."

I crawled back to search for the kit.

In the back corner I found a white plastic first-aid box with a small red cross on the front. It didn't offer much more than a couple of rolls of gauze and some bandages, but at least that was enough for me to wrap Stuart's fingers. That is, if he'd let me. He was still hunched over, cradling his hand and mumbling to himself.

I approached him warily. "Can you let me see?" I shouted. "I want to help."

He just looked through me and shook his head like he was confused.

"Let me see your hand."

He held it out to me. "My finger . . ."

I hated to tell him it was fingers, plural. I just nodded sympathetically. "Can I wrap it?"

He grabbed my hand with his good one and looked at me with wild eyes. "The ring?"

"It's safe." I didn't realize I'd let that slip until the words left my mouth. I held my breath, but Stuart didn't respond at all. I pulled my hand from his grasp. "Let me help you," I yelled. His eyes went vacant as he offered me his hand.

Gingerly, I wrapped what remained of his fingers,

hoping that I was doing it right. Explosions and amputations were not items covered in lifeguard certification.

"Tuck it neatly," he told me.

I blinked at him. "Yeah, okay." At least he was beginning to sound more like his neat-freak self. That had to be a good sign.

I stayed with Stuart for a few moments, just to make sure he was lucid. For such a prissy guy on the outside, he was surprisingly tough when it mattered. He sat stone-faced, his bandaged hand in his lap, taking measured breaths. "Where are we going?" he asked.

"I—I'm not sure." I took a quick look at Ryan. All I had cared about was getting away from Watts. I hadn't even bothered to discuss a destination. "He works in Alaska. Maybe—"

Stuart narrowed his eyes. "We are *not* going to Alaska."

"I'll, um, go talk with him, okay? You going to be all right?"

But Stuart had already tuned me out. He stared vacantly at his hand, muttering to himself.

I crawled forward to talk to Ryan, but noticed that my mom was awake and watching me. I scrambled over to her.

"Hey. How are you feeling?"

She held a hand to her head. "I'm . . . fine. What happened? Where are we?"

"There was an explosion. Ryan helped us escape."

She frowned. "Ryan?"

"We saw him on the docks, remember? He's the guy that lives in your building."

"No, he doesn't."

"But . . ." I shifted uncomfortably. "I met him yesterday. He lives next door to you."

"We ran a check on every resident before we moved in. He was not one of them." Her eyes slid up to the front, where Ryan sat at the controls. "Where did you meet him?"

"On the balcony." My voice was so small it nearly got lost in the drone of the engines.

"Oh, Aphra," she scolded. "You know better than that."

I bit my lip. As much as she made me feel like a naughty six-year-old, she was right. I should know better. Especially after the thing with Hisako at our resort. People are not always what they seem. You can't trust someone you don't know. It's just that Ryan seemed so nice . . . *looked* so nice. Ugh! How could I be such an easy mark?

Stuart crawled over like a three-legged dog to join our huddle. "What is it?"

Mom didn't even have to say anything. Since she and Stuart had worked together, they were probably in tune enough that they were beyond words. She inclined her head toward Ryan and Stuart followed her gaze. He looked back to me. "Where is he taking us?"

"I don't know." He cupped his hand over his ear to illustrate that he couldn't hear me. Plus he probably wanted to make me admit it again, just to rub it in. He needn't have bothered. I knew full well what a complete idiot I'd been. If I had been paying attention, I might have noticed how convenient Ryan's appearance on the docks had been. And how quickly he showed up after the explosion . . . almost as if he knew it was going to happen. He could have planted the bomb himself, to entice us to climb into his plane. And I fell right into his trap. Mom would never have come aboard if she had been conscious. And Stuart . . . he tried to fight it, but we dragged him onto the plane anyway. I hung my head. "I'm sorry."

He regarded me for a moment, then turned to Mom. "I'm going to talk with him."

She shook her head. "Not yet. We haven't—"

"I won't *do* anything," he said. "Just talk. If I can get a reading from the instrument panel, at least we can guess where we're headed."

Seth leaned closer. "What are you guys talking about?" he shouted. I shook my head and pointed up to the cockpit. "What?" he repeated.

I opened my mouth, but I had no words to tell Seth how after everything he had done, after he had come all the way to Seattle to search for his father's ring, I had put him in a plane with someone who might very well want to take that ring away from him. I just shook my head and looked away.

Stuart was crawling unsteadily toward Ryan, which I wasn't convinced was the smartest idea. We had no idea how dangerous he was or who he worked for. My guess was the Mole, since Ryan had helped us escape from Watts, who was CIA. It didn't really matter, since we couldn't trust either one.

Stuart gripped the back of Ryan's seat and hauled himself up. In the shadows, I could make out Ryan's profile as his head turned . . . and Stuart's fist raised. What was he doing?

Seth looked to my mom. "What's happening?"

Before she could answer, the plane banked sharply to the left. Mom was still strapped down, but Seth and I tumbled hard against the wall. He grabbed the net with one arm and me with the other as the plane wobbled again. "What is going on?"

I wished I knew. It had looked to me like Stuart was about to attack Ryan. Maybe Ryan banked to throw Stuart off balance. If that was the case, then Ryan was done pretending to be nice. Whether I wanted to or not, I had to warn Seth. I pulled his head close to mine. "Ryan might be a—"

The plane lurched and dropped and my head smacked right into Seth's nose. He reared back and his arm slipped away from my waist. We banked right this time, the wing almost straight down, and I slid across the floor, slamming into the other wall. Pain shot through my shoulder. I managed to grab on to the securing strap with the other arm and pull myself up. In the cockpit area, Ryan and Stuart were fighting for control over the plane. Neither one was winning.

"We have to help!" I yelled to Seth.

He shook his head and stopped rubbing his sore nose long enough to pantomime that he couldn't hear. I let go of the net and started crawling toward him when I was thrown forward, crashing into the backs of the pilot seats. I tried to pull myself up when the plane climbed and sent me sprawling backward.

Seth grabbed my hand and pulled me back by him and my mom.

"Tie yourself in!" she yelled.

We wrapped the nets and the ties and anything else we could find around us as the plane bucked one last time. The propellers sputtered. The sound of the engines died. My stomach tumbled as the g-force pressed me back against the wall.

"Put your head between your knees!" Mom yelled. "Lock your hands behind your head like this!" She illustrated, lacing her fingers.

I followed her directions, trying to stay as calm as she appeared to be, but my hands shook and tears welled in my eyes.

"We're going to be okay," she yelled.

I nodded, even though I wasn't so sure.

She broke her crash position and gave me a rough hug. "I love you, Aphra," she said hoarsely. "No matter what happens, always remember that."

I hugged her back—for the first time in four years—just before we went down.

CHAPTER
7

The world spun first sideways, then upside down. I clung to the cargo netting, trying to focus only on Seth and my mom as my body slammed into the floor, the ceiling, the wall. If I was going to die, I wanted theirs to be the last faces I saw.

Suddenly we jumped as if we'd been swatted by a giant hand. The plane flipped. Tumbled. Dropped. There was a horrible screeching sound. Crashing. Shattering glass and tearing metal. And then . . . we stopped.

The smell of pine trees and rain and freshly shredded wood filled the plane. Cool air washed over my skin. I craned my neck to see a huge tree branch impaled through the windshield, illuminated by a faint blue light from the instrument panel. I couldn't see Ryan or Stuart.

"Mom?" I nudged her from the snarl of netting we were caught in. She coughed.

"Is she all right?" Seth's voice sounded very close, but I couldn't see him as I hung upside down in the cargo net. I reached back a hand and he brushed my fingers with his. "Are *you* okay?"

"Yeah." And I was. Except that all the blood was rushing to my head, making my eyes bulge and my lips ache.

My pulse throbbed in the bump on my scalp. "Help me get out of this." I started to pull my arm free of the net.

"Careful," Mom said, her voice weak. "There could be glass . . . sharp metal."

Inch by inch I lowered my body to the ceiling of the plane. I helped Mom out of her straps while Seth undid his.

My head was still spinning. "What happened?"

"The pontoons . . . " Mom said. "They must have slowed us down when we hit the trees."

"Hit trees," Seth repeated. He sounded dazed. "We crashed."

"Yes," Mom managed.

We sat still, letting it sink it. All around us it was eerily quiet.

"Where's Stuart?" I asked.

"I don't see him," Seth said softly.

I closed my eyes, imagining him thrown from the plane, his lifeless body lying broken and still on the forest floor. "What about . . . Ryan?"

Seth craned his neck to see around the seats. "He's still strapped in. It looks like there's blood on the glass in front of him. His head probably hit the windshield."

"Do you think he's dead?"

"I don't know."

We let that one sink in, too. And then Mom coughed. "We need . . . to get out. The forest can . . . be dry in August. Flammable. If the plane . . ."

She didn't need to say anything more. Seth sat up straight. "I'll check the door."

"Be careful!" I said. "The glass."

Seth slid, carefully, cautiously, inch by inch to the door. He pushed against it. "It's jammed."

"Try again," I urged.

Seth wrestled with the handle and pushed a shoulder against the door. It didn't budge. "Can we get out through the window? It's already broken."

I chewed my lip and looked to my mom for guidance, but she was quiet and I couldn't see her face very well in the shadows. "I don't know. The glass is pretty jagged. That's probably our last resort for an escape route." I crawled carefully toward him. "I'll help with the door. We're upside down, so the pressure points might be different. Let's try pushing from a different angle."

"I can't even get the handle to budge."

"We'll do it together."

We wrestled with the door until finally the latch gave way. The metal screeched as Seth pushed the door open.

It was unbelievably dark outside. "Where are we?" I whispered.

Seth shivered beside me. "I don't know. I can't see anything."

Which was true. The moon barely managed to break through the clouds overhead, let alone direct its weak light through the tall trees that surrounded us. The only things I could make out were tree trunks and the heavy, bone-chilling mist that drifted in through the cabin door.

It almost made me want to close the door again. Mom had said that the plane could start a fire, but I wasn't so sure. We hadn't set off any sparks yet. Maybe we were okay. Was I willing to risk our lives on a maybe, though? "We should check around the plane. Make sure there's no fuel leaks or anything."

"Maybe we should get your friend out of that chair first," Seth said, pointing to where Ryan dangled upside down from the pilot's seat.

I flinched at his word choice. Ryan was hardly my friend. Not that it really made a difference, but I didn't like the implication. Of course I had earned it.

Seth eyed the gash on Ryan's forehead and the blood that steadily drip, drip, dripped onto the ceiling. "Maybe we should check if he even has a pulse."

I reached up between the seats and felt for Ryan's neck. When I touched him, he moaned. I yanked my hand back. "He's alive."

Seth pulled a face as though disappointed. "Okay. Let's get him down out of that chair."

He reached beneath Ryan to support his weight as I undid the harness. Ryan slumped downward and I grabbed his legs to keep him from falling right on top of Seth.

His foot slipped away and swung down, crashing into the branches.

"Aaaah!" someone cried out.

"Seth! It's Stuart!" I dropped Ryan's legs and dug under the prickly pine branch. "He's wedged under here."

Seth lowered Ryan to the ceiling of the plane and hurried to my side. Together we worked Stuart loose and pulled him from under the branches. Even in the darkness I could tell he was pretty badly scratched up. But at least he was breathing on his own. Since he'd been in the front with no seat belt on when we crashed, that in itself was a miracle.

Everything I knew about first aid said that we should have put both of them on a stiff board before moving them, in case they had hurt their spines. Unfortunately, we had no boards.

I peered into the dark belly of the plane. "Let's take the nets down," I said to Seth. "We can use them to drag these guys clear of the control area so we can help them."

We unhooked the nets and laid a couple of them flat. Carefully, we slid Stuart onto the nets and dragged him to the rear of the plane and then did the same for Ryan.

"How is he?" Mom asked. She sounded groggy.

"He's alive," I told her. Beyond that, I didn't know. "How are you?"

"A little banged up, but fine." She crawled over to where Ryan lay. "Looks like he's lost a lot of blood."

"Head wounds bleed a lot," I said, straightening the nets. "They look a lot worse than they are." In fact, his head looked pretty bad, but I didn't want to think about what that might mean. The first-aid training I had received when I got my lifeguard certification back home only covered so much. "We should probably see if we can stop the bleeding. There was a first-aid kit in here somewhere . . ."

The light from the instrument panel didn't quite reach to the back of the plane, where I had left the kit—not that it would still be there after the way we'd been tossed about. "See if you can find it," I said to Mom. "Seth and I are going to check the plane outside to make sure we're not setting ourselves up to become a giant tiki torch."

Even in the shadows I didn't miss the way her brows raised as I was talking. Whatever. Maybe it was time she got a taste of what it felt like to have someone else tell her what to do.

Seth jumped down from the plane and reached back to help me down. I didn't really need the help, but I appreciated the gesture.

"I can hardly see anything out here," I said. "Can you?"

"Not much." He tightened his grip on my hand. "Where do you think we are?"

"I can't tell. Someplace with really big trees."

"Thanks, Sherlock."

"Maybe we're on a mountain. The ground's sloping pretty steep here. Plus it's cold. Much colder than it was in Seattle. So we're probably at a higher elevation."

"Not bad."

"I try."

"Well, let's get looking, since we can see so well."

We felt our way around the plane. Between the mist and the ground cover and the fact that there was no light to speak of, we pretty much had to. I fell more than once anyway, the ground was so uneven.

I wasn't exactly sure what aviation fuel smelled like, but I didn't smell anything that didn't seem to belong in the woods. As far as we could see, there were no sparks being thrown, there was no imminent danger of fire ... especially since my feet were soggy just from walking around. I couldn't imagine how anything so damp could be tinder dry. Maybe Mom was mistaken. But I wasn't going to tell her that.

When we crawled back into the plane, Stuart was sitting up. He may have been leaning against the wall of the plane for support, but for someone who should by all rights be dead, leaning was remarkable progress.

"What did you find?" he asked. He practically grunted the words.

"Nothing exciting," I said. "How are you feeling?"

"I've been better."

I crawled across the floor. "Where do you hurt?"

His laugh was more of a horrible wheezing sound. "What are you going to do? Fix me?"

"Don't pay any attention to him," Mom said from the shadows. "He's in a lot of pain."

"What's wrong?"

"He may have broken some ribs. Or at the very least bruised them."

"Ouch," Seth said. "That's got to hurt."

Stuart wheezed the awful laugh again, but this time it ended in a spasm of coughing. That must have hurt even worse, judging by the little sobbing noises that followed.

"Isn't there anything we can do to help him?" I asked.

"Yes," Mom said. "We can get him to a doctor."

Ryan could use a doctor, too. And probably Mom. Since she had lost consciousness after the explosion, I worried that she might have a concussion. But first we had to find our way out of the woods. Literally.

"Mom? Do you know how to read the navigation system on one of these things?"

"Most likely. Yes."

"The lights are still on. Do you think . . . ?"

"Not a bad idea." She climbed up front and I followed her. She pressed some buttons and turned some knobs, but apparently whatever she hoped to accomplish didn't happen. She grumbled.

"What is it? What's wrong?"

She shook her head. "No luck. The navi's broken. So is the radio."

"So where *are* we?"

"We couldn't have gone far from Seattle," she said, maybe more to herself than to me, but I jumped on it anyway.

"That's what I was thinking. We couldn't have been in the air more than half an hour."

"True. But I had no orientation from the back of that plane. I can't even guess in which direction we were flying."

"Northeast," Stuart said weakly. "I saw . . . the instrument panel before we went down. We . . . were headed northeast."

"So we're—what? In the North Cascades?" Mom asked.

"That would be . . . my guess," he wheezed. "West side of . . . the pass, judging by the vegetation."

"Where was he taking us?" I wondered aloud.

"More importantly, who was waiting for us at the destination?" Mom cleared her throat. "Seth, the plane's locator device is flashing." She paused meaningfully. "It appears to be working fine."

Seth flinched. "So if Ryan's 'friends' were tracking the plane . . ."

Mom nodded slowly. "If we stay here, they would find us, yes."

"Then we need to get out of here!"

"Wait a second. Hold on." Stuart pushed himself up

on one elbow. "Where would we go? We have no idea where we *are*."

"We're in the mountains, right?" Seth said. "We head downhill and—"

"Downhill which way? We're in the Cascades, son. Mountains in all directions. With no clear sense of location, you could hike for days and end up in some valley *further away* from civilization than when you started."

Panic crossed Seth's face. He didn't have days to wander around in the wilderness. He had to get the ring to his dad. Immediately.

"We could wait till morning," I suggested. "Once we can see what's around us, it'll be easier to get our bearings."

Seth shook his head. "Whoever Ryan's working for isn't going to wait till morning to send someone to look for the plane."

Stuart scoffed. "They'd have to hike in."

"Unless they had a helicopter," I argued.

Mom cut in. "We *should* wait until morning. It's too dangerous to try and climb down in the dark. I've hiked up here before. Even in the light, the vegetation can be deceiving. The ground can drop off suddenly, and if you don't see where you're going, that can spell disaster. Besides, we'd be half frozen before sunrise. We can keep warmer inside the plane. If we hear anyone coming, we can hide before they reach the crash site."

"What?" Seth drew back. "No. We should at least try—"

"Seth, you were out there," Mom said. "Could you see where you were going?"

His shoulders slumped. "No."

"All right, then. We wait for sunrise."

We settled down in a huddle to keep warm. Even with the plane shut tight, the cold crept in, licking at my skin, sending shivers throughout my body. I was glad for the sweatshirt Seth had given me.

Before long, I could hear Stuart snoring softly. Even Seth's breathing settled into a slow, steady rhythm. As tired as I was, I couldn't make myself sleep. I shivered and snuggled closer to my mom. She'd been trying to act tough and in control, but I was worried about her. She'd been knocked out and then banged around pretty good. I couldn't help but notice that she had let me take the lead a couple of times since the crash. That wasn't like her. She could have a concussion. The climb down would not be easy for her.

With his injuries, it would be near to impossible for Stuart. I wondered if maybe there was an alternative to hiking down the mountain. Maybe we could hide and signal for help somehow—although I didn't know how we'd do that without alerting Ryan's friends.

Mom nudged me. "You should try to sleep," she whispered.

"You sleep. I'll take this watch."

"Hon, there's something I learned very early in this game. Sleep whenever you can because you never know when you'll have the chance again. You should get some rest. I'll keep an eye out. I got some sleep earlier."

"You passed out."

"I was resting, nonetheless."

I lay still for a moment, staring into the darkness. "What are we going to do about Ryan?" I whispered.

She didn't answer at first and I thought she had fallen asleep. "What do you mean?"

"When we go. We can't leave him here alone. He could die."

"Well, we can't carry him down the mountain. That would be impossible."

"But he's seriously injured."

"All the more reason not to move him."

"There could be wild animals."

"His people will come for him."

"And if they don't?"

I could feel her stiffen beside me. "Aphra, you have to learn to set priorities and stick with them, no matter the distraction. Sometimes you have to make tough decisions."

My throat felt hot and tight. I swallowed hard. I knew how it felt to be on the receiving end of those tough decisions. Her priority for the past four years had been to search for the Mole's minion. She had given up her family to do so. What did that make me? A distraction?

"Our priority is getting off this mountain," she said firmly. "We can't take him with us."

"I know." I lay silent, snuggling close to her. Beneath the mask of ceramic dust and sweat, she smelled just as I remembered, like white flowers in a meadow. Not exotic island flowers, but sturdy, reliable, mainland flowers. I closed my eyes, trying to store the moment for future memory. Once this was all over, who knew if I would ever see my mom again?

CHAPTER
8

I didn't think it was possible to sleep, but when I opened my eyes, the blackness had turned to gray. I sat up, stiff and cold. My body ached in places I didn't even know were possible. Mom was already awake, as was Stuart. They stood together by the plane's open door.

"It's time," she said. "We should get moving."

Seth had been sleeping beside me—a fact I wished I had realized earlier so that I could have enjoyed it. I nudged him. "Seth—"

He bolted upright, fists tight at his sides. His eyes were wild as he tried to focus on me, and for a moment I thought he really might take a swing at me. "What? What?"

I rubbed his arm—warily, keeping an eye on those fists. "It's morning. We can go now."

Panic crossed his face. I understood without having to ask; the clock was ticking. "What time is it?"

"About four," Mom said. "The sun won't be up for about an hour, but it's light enough to see."

He scrambled to his feet and reached back to help me up. I stood. Sort of. It was too tight in the plane to stand up all the way, so I sort of crouched and followed Seth to the open door.

I looked back one last time before jumping out. In the shadows, I couldn't be sure, but I swear Ryan was watching us leave.

Back home on the island, a rain-forest jungle hugs the back side of the resort. For years, I'd found solitude and solace hiking through the trees. Even so, the forest on the mountain that morning was anything but comforting. It was completely alien to me. Instead of the familiar palm trees and bamboo, I found myself surrounded by thick cedars and tall pines. The understory was so thick that we literally had to fight to get through it.

All around us, shrubs and pines grew so dense that I could barely see ten feet in any direction. Above, the tree cover filtered out the rising sun, and cast everything in shadow. Silence weighted the air. With the ghostly mist swirling around us, it was all too easy to imagine that we had fallen into a haunted wood from which we might never escape.

But we had to. Escape, that is. Seth was running out of time to at least let his dad's captors know he had the ring. We had to get down the mountain. Only the mountain wasn't going to make it easy. Beneath our feet, the ground bunched and fell away, both without warning. The brush looked like it was all about the same height, but beneath it, the ground could have a three-foot drop-off that we might not see until we had fallen and twisted an ankle or worse. And the entire time we hiked, I don't think we came upon a flat surface once. The ground sloped relentlessly downward. I could already feel my toes and heels begin to blister.

Stuart was a mess. He could barely see where he was going without his glasses, for one thing, and with all the blood he'd lost, he wore out easily. Seth practically had to carry him several times just so we could keep moving. So even though I wasn't feeling too great, I wasn't about to complain about blisters and sore feet. They were nothing compared to what Stuart had been through.

Mom and I led the way, clearing the path, each of us whacking back branches with lengths of metal we had pulled from the wreckage. It was hard work and the progress was slow. And it gave me blisters on my hands, to add to a growing list of discomforts I wouldn't complain about.

"We need to find a trail," Mom told me. "Even a deer trail would do. Someplace where the vegetation is worn down. We'll never make it out of here like this."

I agreed, but what could we do until we found such a trail? We kept whacking.

Finally, I had to ask. "How long will it take them?"

"Take who?"

"You said Ryan's people would come to find the wreck."

She hacked at a vine with her makeshift machete. "I don't know." The strain in her voice worried me. "I would assume they were tracking the flight from the moment we left the dock. They may well have been following us."

That left me with a new stab of panic. "So they'd know exactly where we went down. They could be here really soon."

"Yes."

"We have to move faster."

"Yes."

I attacked the brush with a vengeance.

"Nat," Stuart called weakly. "Could we rest for a moment, please?"

I glanced nervously over my shoulder. I wasn't at all sure we should stop. Not yet. We had been fighting our way through the brush for what seemed like hours, but had we covered enough ground to be safe?

But Mom agreed with Stuart. "Yes. Of course. Let's find a spot where we can sit."

We hiked a little farther before Seth spotted a fat log curving up from the mist. Stuart sank onto it with a sigh and leaned back against a tree. He closed his eyes. It was too shadowy to really get a look at his coloring, but the way he rasped in each breath, he *sounded* awful. I wasn't sure how long Stuart would be able to last, wandering around in the forest.

Mom sat next to him. She didn't say anything, just sat there. I wondered if she was thinking the same thing I was about his chances for survival.

Seth motioned to me and we walked a short distance

away, sitting together on a lichen-splotched boulder. "I can't carry him very much farther," he said in a low voice.

"I know. Mom and I can—"

"We should scout ahead and see if we can find a trail or a river or something that will make the hiking easier."

We walked slowly, counting paces and bending branches so that we could find our way back. It wasn't as complicated as it sounds, either, since there was really only one logical direction we could go. We followed the sloping ground downward.

After a while I began to notice more light shining through the tree branches. The trees themselves looked smaller, and spaced farther apart. The smells changed, too. Instead of just mold and damp pine, I caught a whiff of something else, fresh and clean, mingled with . . . I wrinkled my nose. Old fish.

"Do you hear it?" Seth said.

I stood still and listened. Sure enough, from somewhere not too far away came the distinct rush of water. A river.

We had to scout three different routes, but finally, we found our way to the riverbank. After the eerie darkness of the forest, the river was almost mystical, the way the predawn glow caught the water. It also felt like it was a few degrees cooler by the water.

I shivered.

Seth wrapped his arms around me and pulled me close. For the first time since the crash, I felt warm. I rested my head against his chest and let my eyes follow the rush of the river to the valley below. Against a backdrop of jagged, snowcapped peaks, dark, narrow pines rose from the mist, contrasted with splotches of golden yarrow. Under different circumstances, the scenery alone would have taken my breath away. But we weren't on some sightseeing trip. We were there because someone wanted Seth's dad's ring. Wanted it bad enough to kill for it. And, in Ryan's case, perhaps to die for it.

I drew the ring from my pocket and placed it in Seth's hand. "Everything's going to be all right."

He worked his jaw. "It has to be."

I tightened my arms around his waist. For the sake of Seth's dad, I knew we had to find a way to get the ring through to him. But I also knew that as soon as we did, Seth and I would have to say good-bye.

"We should get back," I whispered, even though part of me wanted to stay there forever.

Stuart didn't look much better when we returned to where he was resting. His face was pale except for two bright pink spots, high on his cheeks. Dark circles shadowed his eyes. I wasn't sure how much farther he would be able to go.

"We found a river," I said. "We can follow it."

"Near?" Mom asked.

"Not far. How's Stuart?"

"I'm fine," Stuart said. As if to prove it, he pushed himself up from the log, although he grunted from the effort. He squinted up at the angle of the sun in the small patches of sky we could see through the trees. "It's getting late. We should get moving."

It took twice as long to reach the river with my mom and Stuart as it had when just Seth and I were hiking. By the time we reached the edge of the forest, the sun had swung high in the sky and the last of the mist had burned away.

"We thought maybe we should follow the river," Seth said. "It will be easier to walk out here. Less undergrowth to crawl over." Which was true, but it was also rockier. We'd be climbing more than walking and I wasn't sure how much of that Stuart would be able to take.

Mom had another concern. "We'd also be more visible."

"If we hear a plane or anything, we can run into the trees," Seth assured her. It seemed to make the most sense.

The route proved to be easier, but Stuart still tired quickly. Before long, he had to stop and rest again.

I pulled Mom aside. "How much further do you think we have to go? Stuart lost a lot of blood last night. His ribs must be killing him. And I'm afraid his hand is going to get infected." The gauze that I had wrapped it with was black with dried blood and dirt. We probably should have taken it off altogether, but he was being very protective of his hand. He didn't want anyone to touch it. Besides, I wasn't entirely sure I wanted to look at those fingers again, so I really hadn't tried to pursue the issue.

"We've got to keep his strength up," Mom said. "Wild huckleberries grow in this area. Thimbleberries, too. Maybe we should take a moment to gather some lunch."

The berries grew on long, tangled brambles that left our hands scratched and raw from picking them. Stuart was too weak to be of much help, so Mom and Seth and I gathered what we could and then sat on the rocks with him to eat them.

When we were done—which didn't take long—Seth picked up a small stone and threw it toward the river. "Do you suppose they found him yet?"

"Ryan?" Stuart daintily dabbed the corner of his lips with a grubby finger. "I don't know. I'd think we would have heard the helicopter."

I looked up. "How do you know they'd bring a helicopter?"

"Think about it. They're not going to land a plane up here. We don't know where the nearest roads may be. A helicopter would be the quickest way to the accident site."

"Then why wouldn't they have come last night? If they didn't have to hike in, why would they wait?"

He shrugged. "Maybe that tracking device *wasn't* working," he said blandly. "They may not have been able to see the wreckage until it was light."

"Who do you think he works for?" Seth asked. "The CIA?"

I glanced at Mom. If Ryan was CIA, wouldn't she know it? Besides, Watts was CIA and Ryan had helped us get away from him. But Mom didn't let on that she knew anything.

"He's one of *them*," Stuart said bitterly, and I could only assume he was talking about the Mole and his minions. I know it wasn't really a big reveal—it was the only other alternative—but seeing the look of panic that crossed Seth's face, I wished that Stuart had learned, like my mom, to keep his thoughts to himself.

CHAPTER
9

We heard the helicopter for the first time when the sun hung directly overhead. I almost didn't hear the *thwap-thwap-thwap* of the rotors at all because it was lost in the noise of my mom and me chopping through the brush. Plus the sound was so familiar—I'd heard it almost daily on the island—that it almost didn't register until it was too late.

It was Seth who picked it up first. He froze in his tracks and grabbed my arm. "Wait. What was that?"

"What?"

"That sound?"

I heard it then. "Mom. Listen!"

She stopped her blade midswing and gave me a quizzical look. But then she heard it; I could see the understanding dawn on her face. "Helicopter," she said. "Get down!"

We crouched in the brush and waited for the sound to go away.

We continued our hike in a state of heightened alert. Every noise, every shadow, sent us scurrying back into the tangled underbrush and the trees. But as the afternoon wore on, we began to be less vigilant. Plus, by then we were exhausted. The route we were trying to follow was very nearly impassable. With the exception of the short, fitful rest in the plane, we hadn't slept. And berries can provide only so much energy.

I was becoming clumsy in my fatigue, tripping over my own feet, not to mention the vegetation. My mind was a jumble; I didn't seem to be able to clear my head, but I couldn't quite pin down one thought and stick with it, either.

I was aware enough to be worried about Stuart, though. If I was a mess, Stuart—with his blood loss and bruised ribs—was even worse. He kept muttering things that didn't make sense—although I admit I was beyond trying to figure him out—and was starting to become irritable with Seth when all Seth was doing was trying to help him keep up.

We had all become draggy and unaware when the sound returned.

We'd come to the edge of a steep drop when we heard it, distant at first, but definitely drawing closer. In a cluster, we stumbled into the woods, tripping over vines, getting snagged on the brambles, fighting in vain to make our tired bodies move faster. Once again, we hid in the brush at the base of a huge tree, but this time, we saw the beast.

It was like a scene from an action movie. We huddled in the bushes, barely daring to breathe, when suddenly a black helicopter rose from beyond the hill, the wash of its rotors reaching all the way back to where we crouched, stirring the foliage around us.

The tinted cockpit glass seemed to stare at us like huge, rounded bug's eyes. I'm not sure how long it hovered there—it felt like a long time, but was probably only seconds—before it banked sharply and flew away.

Believe me, that eerie encounter was enough to wake us up. My own awareness returned with a vengeance until I thought I would jump out of my skin at every sound.

"They saw us," Seth said. "We have to get out of here."

"We have no way of knowing what they saw," Mom countered, but I could tell by the way she tensed up that she knew he was right.

"They'll be expecting us to follow the river," Stuart put in. "We need to move deeper into the forest."

"But we can't *move* in the forest," Seth said. "We've got to get out of here!"

I left them to argue and hurried back over to the top of the hill. I thought I had seen something and I wanted to be sure.

Mom followed me. "What is it?"

"Down there," I said, pointing. I wasn't sure she saw it at first, but then her eyebrows rose. From a clearing at the bottom of the hill, a couple of thin plumes of smoke rose, curling in the air.

"Campers," she said.

"Campers," I agreed. "They could be our ticket out of here."

● ● ●

To ease Stuart's mind, we took the hard way down, through the woods. I tried to help him as much as possible so Seth wouldn't end up having to carry him again. Still, Seth did most of the heavy lifting, and by the time we reached the bottom of the hill, he was shaking with fatigue.

"You should rest," Mom told him. "You, too, Stuart. Aphra and I will scout ahead."

Seth didn't even argue, and that worried me.

"We'll be right back," I assured him.

We hiked back toward the river.

"You have a plan, I take it?" Mom asked.

"A plan?"

"Right. Talk me through your thought process."

I blinked at her. Since when did she want to hear what I thought? "Okay . . . the way I figure it is that these campers had to get in somehow. They either hiked, drove, or rafted. I don't think they would have hiked, so that leaves driving or rafting, so—"

"Why don't you think they hiked?"

I stopped and looked at her. Was she serious? "Well, because *we* have been hiking all day, *without* schlepping along camping equipment, and it has not been enjoyable. I can't imagine anyone choosing to put themselves through that."

"Maybe they know the trails."

"All right. Fine. Let's say hiking is a possibility, too. Still, there could be a truck . . ."

"And if there is? What would we do, ask for the keys?"

I shook my head. "Wow. You're really supportive."

"I just want to know if you've thought it out."

"Well, I haven't, okay? I've had just about as much time to work this out as you have. Do *you* have any great plans you'd like to share?"

"Don't be snide, Aphra. It doesn't become you."

"Well, I'm sorry. When I get attacked, that's how I react." I stomped ahead of her.

"Who's attacking you?"

I spun around. "Do you *hear* yourself? All this questioning, criticizing. What do *you* call that?"

"Is that what you think this is?"

"Um, hello. Yeah. You treat me like a little kid who doesn't know what to think."

"When I saw you last, you *were* a little kid."

"Well, I've changed since then. But not as much as you have."

She actually looked stung, as if she had no idea. "What are you talking about?"

"Oh, come on." I eyed her up and down. "You're not the same person at all. We used to have fun together. Life was a big adventure. Now I don't even know you anymore. You've become this uptight, pinch-lipped government *agent*."

She bristled. "Aphra, don't be unfair."

"Unfair? That's pretty funny coming from you. You

made me think you and I were a team and then you *left*. Now all I want is a little support, and you can't even give me that."

"I do support you," she said, voice softening, "but this is not a game, Aphra. You need to be sure in your actions. Decisive. That's why I'm challenging you, to make you stronger. To be the smart and tough young woman I raised you to be."

"Raised?" I stepped back. "How could you raise me when you were never there?"

I wished I could take the words back when I saw the tears in her eyes, but I was too hurt to tell her that. I folded my arms and turned away.

She approached me slowly, reached out tentatively, rubbed my arm gently. "I'm so sorry, Aphra. I . . . I should have been there for you. I hope you understand I just wanted to protect you."

"And I wanted a mom."

"I'm here now."

I wiped a stray tear from my cheek. The anger had passed like a summer storm and all I felt now was regret. "I'm sorry for messing things up."

"Oh, no, no." She pulled me into her arms. "You haven't messed up, Aphra. I handled things all wrong."

"But if it wasn't for me—"

"If it wasn't for you, I'd have nothing to fight for. If it wasn't for you, I'd have given up long ago."

I think we both cried ourselves out, standing by the

river. If given a choice, I don't think I would have chosen the route I'd taken, but in the end, I'd do it again without hesitation. I had found what I'd been looking for. I found my mom.

CHAPTER
10

After we had dried our eyes, Mom and I scoped out the origin of the smoke I had seen from atop the hill. Sure enough, downriver we found a campsite. We didn't get too close, just near enough to see the tents and campfire through the trees. Then we hiked back double time to where Seth and Stuart were resting. I waited for Mom to tell them about our discovery, but she looked to me and nodded, giving me the lead.

"We think we might be able to locate some transportation," I began.

Seth's eyes lit up. It was the first encouraging thing he'd heard all day. "Where?"

"We don't *know* that we'll find anything," I said, "but there are some campers down the river. We figure they might have a car or a raft . . ."

Stuart shook his head. "No. We shouldn't be involving civilians. This could get dangerous."

I couldn't help it. I laughed right in his face. Was he kidding? It *could* get dangerous? We'd passed the realm of possibility and landed smack in the middle of absolute certainty about twenty hours ago. Had he not looked at his hand lately?

"We won't involve the people," Mom said firmly.

"Only the transportation." She raised a hand to stop my protest. "*If* they happen to possess any."

Seth, of course, was more than ready to take the gamble. Stuart kept mumbling and complaining the entire time. If it wasn't for the need to cut him some slack for being injured and all, I would've liked to slap him. As it was, I had to settle for tuning him out.

By the time we neared the camp, long shadows stretched out from the trees and the chill had returned to the air. Shivering, I tried to pick up the pace as much as I could, considering Stuart's inability to keep up. I just figured that the faster we moved, the warmer we'd be. Plus, the quicker we found a way out of there, the sooner we could put the whole thing behind us.

Wood smoke hovered with the gathering mist, and the smell of roasting meat made my stomach rumble.

"What if we just told these people that we needed help?" Seth whispered. "Wouldn't that be easier?"

Mom shook her head. "There would be too many questions we couldn't answer. The fewer explanations needed, the better."

I liked Seth's idea of asking for help, especially if we could share the fire and the food, but Mom was right. Plus I knew from personal experience that a person could be placed in deadly trouble by getting involved. We couldn't impose that danger on anyone.

Men's voices carried through the evening air, and we skirted the perimeter of their camp, keeping out of their way. I spotted four of them on the other side of some green domelike tents, sitting around a campfire, drinking and laughing. Since we didn't see any cars or even tire tracks, we continued on to the river, hoping for a boat.

Sure enough, up on the rocky bank sat two kayaks. My heart dropped. Two. I'd been hoping for a raft or something on which we could all ride out together. With two, we'd have to split up.

As I'd expected, Mom suggested that she and I ride together, leaving Seth once again to take care of Stuart's deficiencies. Between his injured hand and aching ribs, there was no way Stuart could paddle a kayak with any effectiveness, so Seth would have to do enough paddling for both of them.

"It shouldn't be difficult since we will be following the river downstream," Mom assured him. "You sit in the back so you can do the steering."

"I know," Seth said. "I've been kayaking before."

"So have I," I put in—as if it were relevant.

I'd actually only been sea kayaking, and never tandem. Plus these kayaks were built a little differently from what I was used to—wider and a bit shorter, without the upswept bow of the island kayaks. But a kayak was a kayak, I figured. How hard could it be?

While the guys slid their kayak into the water, Mom held ours steady so that I could climb to my seat. I settled down into the cockpit and readied my paddle. She pushed away from the shore before slipping into her own seat.

I held my paddle just above the water until she gave the signal. She counted until we found a rhythm and then instinct took over. I dug deep, pushing the water behind us as fast as I could in order to catch up with Seth and Stuart. The kayak cut through the water like an arrow, racing over the dips and swells. Before long, my arms burned and my shoulders tightened, but I tried not to think about it. Even though my body craved rest, my mind still yelled, *Go! Go!* Cold mountain air snaked across the bow, rippling the fabric of my shirt, blowing back my hair and raising goose bumps on my skin, but all I could think about was getting down the river, away from locator beacons and helicopters. We couldn't paddle fast enough.

I heard rough water as we came toward a bend in the river. That couldn't be good. I tensed and called behind me, "Mom?"

"I hear it."

"What do we do?"

By now, I could see the froth kicking up in the river ahead of us. Each stroke brought us closer. My hands gripped the paddle so hard that I swore I was going to go right through the wood. "Mom?!"

"We'll ride it out! I'll do the steering," she shouted. "You just tell me if you see any major obstacles."

The current pulled us downstream and I soon found that I was using the paddle more for keeping upright than for actual paddling. Icy water sprayed in my face and drenched my hair and clothes. My fingers throbbed from the cold.

I tried to navigate through the worst of it, yelling back to Mom, "Right! Left!" but still we hit rocks under the water, teeth-jarring hits that sent us reeling to the side or shot us into the air, only to slap back down onto the surface to be drenched all over again.

I blinked away water, shivering so hard that my back ached. My arms felt heavy. My head felt thick. That could be why I wasn't quick enough to tell my mom about the huge boulder sticking up from the water until we were right upon it. I did manage to scream, but not until the bow cracked against the boulder, rebounding and spinning us completely around.

Mom fought for control, but we were shooting down the rapids backward. There's not much she could have done. I'm not sure exactly what happened next, but my guess is that the stern hit another rock. Only this time instead of spinning the kayak, it sent it end over end. I shot up in the air. The paddle flew from my hands, but I barely spared it a thought, because I was headed face-first into the river. I pushed free of the cockpit and splashed down ahead of the kayak.

Freezing water closed over me.

My first instinct was to try to swim against the current,

but I did remember from preparing for the whitewater trip—you know, the one with Mom that never happened all those years ago—that if you were thrown from a boat, you were supposed to sit back, try to ride the current feetfirst, and cross your arms against your chest. This rule, of course, presupposed that you were wearing a life vest to keep your head above the water, and maybe a helmet to keep from cracking your skull on a rock. I kept going under and getting a mouthful of water every time I went down. I lost track of Mom and the other kayak. All I could think about was finding the next breath of air and not smashing into anything. That was plenty. Once the river calmed down, I could worry about little things like hypothermia and being stranded alone in the woods.

More than once, my feet smacked into underwater rocks and I was thrown out of position and had to fight to maintain the posture. It was during one of these fights that I hit my tailbone on a rock. Pain flared up my spine and down both legs. I could hardly move. My head dragged under the waves. Water shot up my nose. I gagged and coughed, fighting to keep my head up.

Finally, we came to a bend in the river and the water quieted just a bit. The current was still strong, but at least I was able to gain some control.

I turned around. Where was Mom? All I could see was dark water, swirling, frothing.

"Aphra! Over here!" Stuart and Seth stood knee-deep in the water, making big arm gestures and yelling at me to swim to shore. Their kayak lay on the rocky bank. Apparently they had managed to avoid getting tossed into the water.

Seth cupped his hands around his mouth and yelled something to me, but his voice was lost in the roar of the river.

"Where's my mom?" I yelled.

He shouted something else and pointed.

I almost missed seeing her float by me. Her hand flailed above the water, but in the darkness it almost looked like a jumping fish. But then I saw her face surface. She gasped for air and went under again.

"Mom!"

The current pulled her away from me and I had to swim after her. In the cold, my arms and legs were weighted. It felt like I was swimming through sludge. Frozen, moving sludge. "Mom! Mom!"

Her head popped to the surface a yard or so ahead of me. It took almost all the energy I had left to reach her. I grabbed the back of her shirt. In her panic, she grasped at me and pulled us both under. I fought to get free and pulled away, almost losing her in the current again.

"Relax!" I yelled. "Hold still!"

Never before had I been so grateful for my lifeguard training. I didn't have to think about it; instinct took over. I pushed her so that she was floating on her back and hooked an arm around her torso. With every ounce of strength I had left, I swam with the other arm for the shore. As hard as I pulled, though, I didn't even seem to be moving. The current sucked at us both, carrying us farther downstream.

Seth yelled and splashed through the water, running along the shore to keep up with us. I kept my focus on him and swam harder. He jumped into the water as I got closer and swam out to meet us. Together, we dragged Mom in.

She coughed and gagged, but at least she was breathing on her own. We staggered onto the shore, shivering, legs wobbling. Even though we were out of the water, I knew we weren't home free. The sun had dipped behind the mountains, taking with it what warmth it had provided. We were wet. We were cold. We were lost. We were in big trouble.

"A-Aphra," Mom said between shivers. "I had n-no idea you c-could do that."

"Look!" Stuart cried, pointing downstream. "Lights!"

There were lights, and a lot of them. Maybe a town? I guessed they were about a mile away. I just hoped we could make it that far.

We never got a chance to find out.

Before we had gone ten yards, a black truck crested the hill above us, its bright headlights sweeping down on us and capturing us like some kind of freeze ray.

"You're a hard crew to find," a man's voice called out. "We'd about given you up for dead."

CHAPTER
11

It was over. There was no place to run except back into the river, and that hadn't worked out so well the first time. I grasped Mom on one side and Seth on the other and waited for the inevitable.

The man trotted down the hill toward us, his dark shape backlit by the headlights behind him. "Don! They're soaking wet! We need more blankets!"

I tried to focus on him, but he shined a flashlight in my eyes and I couldn't see anything but white light. "Pupils responsive!" he yelled, and wrapped a heavy, coarse blanket around me.

"You're lucky we saw you," he said as he moved on to Mom. "We had just about called off the search for the night."

"What?"

"The search. We've had crews out all day looking for you. You must have seen them. They spotted you this afternoon, but by the time they called in your location and got bodies up there, you were gone."

Spotted us . . . the helicopters . . .

Ranger Don—I assumed they were both rangers since they were dressed in matching uniforms like overgrown

Boy Scouts—harrumphed. "What were you trying to do, anyway? Get yourself killed?"

"It's a good thing those anglers radioed when their kayaks went missing. Least we knew to check the river."

"The crash site," I said. "Did you find—"

"Let's get you back to the station and your bodies warmed up and then we can talk."

"Station?"

"The ranger station. The quicker we get there, the quicker you can get dry."

Mom and Stuart sat on opposite ends of the middle bench seat in the rangers' SUV, and just behind them, Seth and I huddled together in the far back. Once we weren't moving, the shivering set in for real and we needed each other's body heat, even if there wasn't much to go around.

The whole scenario had a very surreal feel to it; one minute we're fighting our way through the wilderness and the next we're riding along all warm and comfortable on a cushy seat with Bach on the radio. Well, maybe not *completely* comfortable—the SUV bumped and bounced over the rocky terrain, throwing us around pretty good in the back. That, plus the itchy wool blankets they had given us smelled like wet farm animals and . . . well, it seemed strange to be worried about such mundane comforts when just a short while ago I wasn't even convinced we were going to make it down the mountain alive.

When we reached the ranger station, Ranger Don and the first ranger, whose name I never did get, ushered us up the wooden stairs and inside, clucking over us like a couple of old hens. It wasn't until the door closed behind us that I noticed the blond man in the dark suit seated behind the desk.

"Thank God," he said. "We've been looking all over for you."

My face went numb as Watts's cold eyes swept over us.

"They were down by the river, sir," Ranger Don reported. "Just as you predicted."

Watts stood. He planted his hand at his waist, pushing back his jacket enough that his shoulder holster was plainly visible. You know, just in case we forgot who was in control. "Thank you for your outstanding effort today, gentlemen. We couldn't have done it without you." Then, turning to us, "We have some dry clothing and blankets in the next room. And I understand you're in need of medical attention."

"We're fine," I blurted, even though Stuart seriously needed a doctor for his hand. It made me sound like a petulant little kindergartner, but I couldn't stand the way Watts was acting all benevolent.

"I'm glad to hear that," Ryan said from the doorway. "I was worried about you."

My breath caught. I should have known. His head was bandaged and he wore a dark suit and tie similar to the one Watts had on. So, Stuart had been wrong; Ryan was CIA after all. And Stuart had been wrong about leaving Agent Ryan behind at the crash site, too. If we'd taken him with us, he wouldn't have been able to alert Watts about our condition or our whereabouts. Of course we wouldn't have made it very far trying to carry Ryan as well as Stuart, either, so I don't know what choice we had, but it made me feel better to be angry at Stuart, so I wasn't going to analyze it too closely.

"Ladies, you may have the room first," Ryan said, bowing his head in our direction. "Please change quickly. The men should get out of their wet things as soon as possible."

My legs shook so badly that I could hardly follow Mom into the back room. As if practically freezing outside wasn't enough, just being in the same room with Watts again made my blood run cold. I wanted to scream. My mind went back to the chase after Joe died—had that only been a day and a half ago? Watts *had* been following me. He followed me to the apartment. He was following me still. Would I ever be free from him?

I couldn't believe that everyone else was being so calm! Well, maybe I could understand Ranger Don and the other ranger. They probably didn't even know what was going on. I doubt Watts and Ryan announced that they were from the CIA, that they'd killed Joe, and that the rest of us were probably expendable, too. But what was Mom thinking? She hardly even blinked as we passed Ryan in the short hallway leading to the small back room. Were we just going to blithely allow them to herd us wherever they wanted us to go? We had to get out of there. Seth's dad was depending on it.

In the room was a pile of gray sweatpants and sweat-shirts folded on a chair. On top of that sat two plastic Fruit of the Loom packages. I picked one of them up and recoiled. Underwear. One set of women's, one set of men's. I didn't know what was creepier, the thought of putting on underwear that one of those guys out there had bought or going commando under the sweats. I reasoned that the underwear was in a sealed package and the sweats were not, so I'd go with the extra layer. I ripped open the package and gingerly removed a pair, passing the others to Mom. The sweats were all men's size large, so they were huge on us, but at least they were warm.

"What now?" I asked in a small voice as I pulled the sweatshirt over my head.

Mom raised a finger to her lips and looked to the door. Of course. We couldn't talk in there. We couldn't talk anywhere near Watts or Ryan. Somehow we had to figure out a way to communicate, because I didn't intend to go down without a fight.

I pushed up the sleeves and rolled the pant legs so that I wouldn't trip on them and hurried out to the other room. I noticed that Stuart's hand had been freshly bandaged, but he still looked miserable. Seth caught my eye as I entered the room, and then glanced down at his hand. It was curled into a tight fist. I wasn't sure what he was trying to tell me. To fight? I slid a glance at Watts, who had apparently been watching me.

"I hope you found everything you needed," he said smoothly.

"Almost," I said, probably not anywhere near as smoothly, though I was trying to keep my voice steady. "You wouldn't happen to have any shoes and socks up here, would you? My feet are freezing."

He almost didn't bother to hide his smile. Of course they wouldn't give us shoes and socks. Barefoot, we were less of a flight risk. "Please forgive the oversight. We'll find you appropriate footwear when we get to town."

Somehow, I didn't find that comforting.

Mom came out of the room behind me. I couldn't help but think how appropriate it was that our matching gray sweats looked like prison issue.

"Stuart, Seth, why don't you go put on your dry clothes now that the ladies are done," Watts said. I could practically *see* the smirk in his voice.

Seth looked at me again, eyes boring into me, willing me to understand. I caught the movement of his fist once more, before he dropped it to his side.

His fist. The ring. Of course. He'd have no place to hide it while he was changing. I blinked and made myself look away. I didn't make eye contact with him at all as he followed Stuart to the back room, but I managed to stand just close enough that he bumped into me as he passed. He pressed the ring into my hand. I slipped it onto my thumb and made a fist around it, letting the long sleeve of the sweatshirt fall down over my fingers.

The first ranger offered Mom and me some hot coffee. "It'd do good to raise your core temperature."

I snorted and looked over at Watts. No way was I drinking any coffee he'd been anywhere around. Not after seeing what had happened to Joe. I shook my head no.

Finally, once everyone was dressed and warmed and Stuart's vital signs had been checked, Watts announced our departure.

"Gentlemen, thank you again," he said to the rangers. "You have done us a great service today."

They way the two of them beamed, I had to wonder what kind of story Watts and Ryan had told them. As I watched the exchange and their innocent reaction to it, I began to think that they might just be our best allies in this situation. They didn't know what Ryan and Watts were up to. Okay, I didn't know what Ryan and Watts were up to, either, but I knew it wasn't good. If I could just remove the blinders from their eyes, they might be willing to help us escape.

The one thing I couldn't do was leave that ranger

station. Once we were alone with the CIA boys, how would Seth ever get away? He was running out of time.

Watts opened the door. I looked desperately to the naive park rangers, screaming in my head, *Don't let them take us!* They were not tuned in to my telepathy.

What else could I do? I clutched my stomach and doubled over. "Ugn!"

Mom wrapped an arm around my waist. "Aphra, what is it?"

"I don't feel so good," I said weakly. "I . . . need to use the restroom."

Watts rolled his eyes, but how could he refuse me in front of the rangers? He nodded—as if I had been asking his permission!—and pointed out the door to the loo. I hurried inside and locked it behind me.

The bathroom was a dismal little space that looked as if it had seen better days. I curled my toes in disgust at the feel of the cool, somewhat damp tiles beneath my bare feet. I didn't even want to think of the kinds of diseases I could get from direct skin contact. The floor was cracked and yellowed—by age, I hoped—and the toilet in the corner leaned a bit to the left. The single bulb hanging from the ceiling cast an ocher pall over it all.

Worst of all, the place seriously stank of old plumbing and stale pee. I considered cracking open the window, but I didn't want Watts and Ryan to think I was trying to sneak out and come barging in on me. I wasn't going to. Sneak out, that is. Even though I would have loved to put as much distance between Watts and myself as humanly possible, I wasn't going to leave my mom and Seth. Okay, or Stuart, either, even though he had really started to grate on me. I just couldn't do it. Besides, if I did run away, where would I run *to*? No, I would stay put, but I had to find a way to leave a message for the rangers.

I turned in a slow circle, looking for something—anything—I could use to write with, but the bathroom was as depressingly bare as it was filthy. The only decor besides the sink and toilet was an empty paper-towel dispenser, a cracked mirror, and a framed portrait of Smokey the Bear. I am not kidding.

Nothing to write on. Nothing to write with. I chewed the inside of my cheek. There had to be *something* I could do. I looked at the mirror again. A spiderweb of cracks fanned out from the corner as if something—a head or a fist or similar—had smacked it. All I needed was one sliver. Maybe I could scratch a message on the wall or something.

I picked at the edge of the mirror with my fingernails, trying to pry up a piece of glass. It was one of those old drugstore numbers, glued to a cardboard backing, which not only shadowed the reflection just a bit, but also made it supremely hard to pull off a shard without destroying your fingernails. Finally, I was able to work a piece loose.

5

Someone banged on the door. "Are you all right in there?"

I couldn't tell whose voice it was. "Um, yes. I'll be right out." I flushed the toilet for effect.

It didn't work. The banging continued.

"Hold on!" I started to scratch at the wall with the broken piece of mirror, but barely made a letter before the doorknob rattled. I spun away from my SOS, curling my fist around the shard from the broken mirror.

The door swung open and Ryan crowded through the doorway. His gaze flicked past me to the wall. If he noticed my pathetic scratches, it didn't show in his bland expression. "We need to be going now," he said. He steered me out to the porch, where the others were waiting.

Seth shot me a look, eyes wide and questioning. I gave him the slightest shake of my head. I would say that I was trying to act normal, but normal left the building the minute I'd set foot in Seattle. The best I could do was to not fidget so that I wouldn't draw attention to the glass in my hand.

"Let's move," Watts growled. He yanked my mom's arm, pulling her down the porch steps.

Seth jumped forward to defend her, but Stuart held him back with his good hand. He shook his head, pantomiming a gun with his finger, cocking it with his thumb.

Ryan prodded Seth and Stuart forward. I managed to

hang back long enough to tug on Ranger Don's sleeve. "Help us. Please," I said in a low voice.

"That's all right, little lady. It was our pleasure," he said.

"No. I mean, we need—"

Ryan returned to my side and slid a hand around my elbow. "Come, Aphra. Let's not keep Agent Watts waiting."

Watts made my mom sit with him in the front seat of a black Escalade. He put Seth, Stuart, and me—in that order—in the middle seat and Ryan behind us, again with a great show of his gun.

The result was that we couldn't talk to one another without one of them knowing. I stared out the window, watching the moonlit mountain scenery slip by. Someday, I thought, I'd like to come back and visit the Cascades when I could actually enjoy it. If I lived that long.

My fingers throbbed from picking at the glass. A fat lot of good that had done. I ran my thumb over the sharp edge of the sliver of mirror in my hand, trying to come up with a better idea. Outside, the mist had turned to a fine rain, making the road and the trees and the plants around us shine in the weak moonlight.

"Where are you taking us?" Mom asked, her voice nearly lost in the hum of the tires and the *squee-squee-squee* of the windshield wipers.

Watts's eyes never left the road. "Does it matter?"

I exchanged a glance with Seth. Of course it mattered. Why wouldn't it matter?

"You can't go back to your apartment, as I'm sure you know," Watts continued. "That has been sterilized."

Mom didn't say anything.

"You could always publicly return to the Agency, you know. You and I made a good team."

I blanched at the thought.

Mom's voice was monotone. "A rogue agent has no team."

"You're not a rogue, Natalie." He gave her a sideways glance and smiled. It made my stomach turn. "Ooh. You meant *me*. Valuable lesson, Natalie; learn to play the game."

She pressed her lips together and turned her head so that I couldn't see her face anymore.

Watts chuckled and drummed his fingers on the steering wheel. I closed my hand around the glass until it bit into my skin. How I wanted to rake it across his face and wipe that smirk from his lips!

Seth caught my eye and made a face like he was asking me what we should do. I made the same questioning face back. What *could* we do? There were more of us, but they had the gun. Maybe two, if Ryan was packing, which he probably was now that he was all suited up and official. Plus Stuart didn't really count for our side because he was on the injured-reserve list. So we had three against two plus the guns. Not good odds, but something told me that our odds would become even worse once we got to wherever we were going. If we were to have any chance of escaping, we had to take it before we reached our destination.

We couldn't signal Mom to be a part of whatever we might do, which meant it was up to Seth and me. I slid the hand holding the glass shard forward and opened my palm just enough to show him. Problem was, in the shadows, I don't think he saw it. At least if he did, he didn't show any reaction, which I suppose was very clever, but it didn't help me much. I looked down at my hand then back up again like he'd done with the ring. Down and up, down and up. *Come on, Seth, get the message.*

He gave me an exasperated, wide-eyed stare as if to say, *Yeah, I got it. So what are we going to do with it?*

Heck if I knew.

And we never got a chance to find out, because all of a sudden Stuart snatched the glass shard from my hand, and in one fluid movement he swung his good hand back, slicing Ryan across the cheek, as he slammed the elbow of his other arm against the back of Watts's head, knocking him out cold. Watts swerved into the oncoming lane. Twin spots of light raced toward the car. A horn blasted. Mom reached over and jerked the steering wheel the other way. We smashed into the guardrail and rebounded, spinning almost a complete three-sixty before coming to a stop. Watts's head came to rest on the steering-wheel horn, provoking a sustained, three-toned wail.

"Grab his gun," Stuart yelled, pointing back at Ryan. But Ryan wasn't incapacitated. He was angry. He reached for his gun before Seth or I could grab it.

"I wouldn't do that if I were you," Stuart said. In his hand he held Watts's gun, and pointed it right at Ryan's head.

CHAPTER
12

"**H**ands where I can see them," Stuart ordered. "Seth, grab his gun."

"Seth, don't do it," Ryan growled.

"The gun, Seth!"

Seth hesitated, but finally reached back and took Ryan's gun from its holster.

"You don't know what you're doing, kid."

Seth tightened his grip on the gun. He couldn't quite bring himself to point it at anyone, though, or to put his finger on the trigger, I noticed.

"Okay, now everyone out of the car," Stuart ordered.

No problem there. I couldn't get out of Watts's car fast enough. The ground was cold and wet and the gravel bit into my bare feet, but I didn't care. I finally felt like I could breathe again.

Seth climbed from the car as Stuart held the gun on Ryan.

Without taking his eyes off Ryan, Stuart motioned with his bandaged hand to Seth. "Lemme see that thing. Is it even loaded?"

Seth furrowed his brows, turning the gun over in his hands. Stuart snatched it with his three good fingers. "Worthless!" He threw it to the other side of the road, where it skittered across the asphalt. The wheel of a passing car caught the gun and twirled it on the road like some macabre game of spin the bottle. The muzzle slowly came to a stop—pointed back at us.

Mom jumped out and ran to my side. "Are you all right? What was that? What's happening?"

"It's okay. I'm fine," I assured her.

Stuart made Watts and Ryan get out of the SUV with their hands clasped behind their heads. He ordered them to kneel on the wet road while Seth frisked them to make sure they weren't carrying any other weapons. If I didn't thoroughly dislike Watts, I might have felt sorry for the guy. He looked so confused . . . and chagrined for having been overcome in front of both his former and current partners—by a guy with one good hand, no less.

Once he was sure they didn't have any weapons, Stuart allowed them to stand.

"Why the hell'd you hit me?" Watts demanded, rubbing the back of his head.

"Effect," Stuart said. "Get the ring."

My head spun. They were *together*?

Watts stepped up to Seth and stuck out his hand. "Give me the ring, kid."

Mom gasped. "You! Both of you! How could you, you dirty—"

"Ah, ah, ah." Stuart pointed the gun at her. "Watch that temper, Nat."

Watts poked his finger in Seth's chest. "The ring!" he demanded.

Seth didn't even flinch. "I don't have it."

"Of course you have it," Stuart snapped. "Your little girlfriend here told me all about it."

Seth shot me a disbelieving look and I shook my head wildly. I wanted to deny telling Stuart about the ring, but that seemingly insignificant moment on the plane came back to me all too clearly.

"You knew the kid had the ring all this time?" Watts sniped. "Why didn't you just take it and save us all this trouble?"

"I needed them to get me off the mountain," Stuart said simply.

"Stuart." Mom's voice shook. "Why are you doing this?"

He laughed humorlessly. "Well, it's like my daddy used to say: 'Son, keep your friends close and your enemies closer.'"

"Enemies? But . . . we're on the same side."

Stuart laughed and I have to say, it was about the ugliest sound I've ever heard. "Well, you got that wrong."

"But . . . why?"

"You were getting too close. I joined you and Joe to keep an eye on you, Nat."

"We were right, then. The Mole had someone inside the Agency."

"No, you were wrong. The Mole has *several* someones."

"And you are one of them."

"Bingo."

"But how could you?" Mom exclaimed. "What about Joe? Did you kill him?"

Stuart laughed again. The sound made my stomach turn. "Not personally, no."

Mom looked stung. "Damian?" she said, calling Watts by his first name. "*You* killed him?"

"I got bills to pay, Natalie. I'm gonna give my services to the highest bidder."

"But why? Why Joe? Why not—"

Stuart laughed humorlessly. "He found something, Nat. A list of names on that ring of young Romeo's here. That's why he wanted you to meet him. He discovered a name on the ring that I could not afford to have revealed. Mine."

The confusion lingered in her eyes. "Your name was on that list? You mean . . . you're a sleeper? But . . . your parents!"

"Yes, that was a nice touch, wasn't it? Their deaths went a long way toward convincing the Agency to embrace me. Who better to trust than some poor kid whose parents were killed by the Bad Guy?"

"What are you saying? You killed your own parents?"

"They defected. *They* chose their demise."

I stared at him in horror. Suddenly he wasn't the annoying and pathetic nerd anymore. He was a monster. And if he was the kind of person who would kill his own parents, we were in deep trouble.

The monster turned to Seth. "Give the man the ring, kid."

"I. Don't. Have. It."

Stuart was not amused. He gave Watts a look and then nodded at me. Watts grabbed my arm and yanked me forward. Stuart shoved the cold gun barrel against my scalp and drew the hammer back with a click. "One more time, kid. Where's the—"

"Don't shoot!" I cried. "He really doesn't have it! I swear."

"Start talking." He pressed the metal harder and harder into my skin until I winced.

"He gave it to me. Before the river. H-he didn't have any pockets and I did, so he gave it to me to hold!"

Stuart raised a brow and looked at Seth. "Is that true?"

Lie, Seth. Lie!

"Yeah, I gave it to her."

"Well," Stuart drawled. "Isn't that nice." He lowered the gun. "Aphra, sweetheart, I need you to give me the ring."

"I—I don't have it anymore."

Watts grabbed a handful of my hair and yanked my head back. As if that wasn't painful enough, Stuart jammed the gun against my cheek. "I'm going to ask you one last time—"

"Stop! Stop this!" Mom jumped toward me. "You leave her alone!"

Watts backhanded her and sent her sprawling onto the pavement. She tried to get up and he kicked her down again. She lay still. Rage poured out of me. I didn't even think of the consequences. I wrenched away from Watts's grip and jumped on him like a cat on fire, clawing, biting, spitting. He threw me to the ground, but I got some pretty good licks in first.

Watts pulled back his foot to kick me, too. I rolled to the side, drawing my legs up and covering my head with my hands. Then something exploded. Watts dropped to the ground, screaming and holding his knee. Blood oozed from between his fingers.

"Oh, be quiet." Stuart sneered and lowered the gun. "One thing I cannot abide is a man who loses control." He held up his bandaged hand with the missing fingers. "I'd say we're even now."

Leaving Watts to whimper on the ground, Stuart turned to me again. "You see, Aphra? I'm losing my patience. Please give me the ring."

"I swear, I don't have it. I lost it when I got tossed from the kayak!"

"Oh, really." He pointed the gun straight at Seth. "I'm through playing games. You have until the count of three to tell me the truth. One . . ."

"Wait!" I scrambled to my feet.

Seth looked at me with wild eyes, shaking his head no. I knew he was afraid to lose the ring for fear of losing his dad, but the way I saw it, if Seth was dead, his dad would be dead, too.

"No, please!" I pleaded. "It's at the bottom of the river, Stuart! If I could give it to you, I would—"

"Two . . ."

"Wait! I'm sorry! I'm sorry! I have it!"

Seth's shoulders slumped.

"Please," I cried. "Don't hurt him." I pulled the sweat-shirt sleeve back and slid the ring slowly from my thumb.

"Aphra, no," Seth whispered.

I couldn't look at him, couldn't bear to see the defeat on his face. I kept my eyes on Stuart and held the ring out to him. He took the ring in his bandaged hand. Looked down.

That was all I needed. I kicked up and out and caught him square in the stomach. Not that I have a powerful roundhouse or anything, but with his hurt ribs, it was enough to make him stumble backward, off balance. Ryan flew at him and grabbed Stuart's injured hand, twisting his arm behind his back until he dropped to his knees. The gun clattered to the road. Ryan kicked it away.

"Down on the ground!" he yelled, twisting Stuart's arm higher. He forced Stuart facedown onto the concrete.

Seth jumped in then, peeling Stuart's fingers back one by one until he let go of the ring.

"Aphra!" Mom yelled.

I had been so intent on the fight that I hadn't noticed Watts drag himself toward Stuart's discarded gun. I pounced on the gun and scooped it up. It felt cold and awkward and *wrong* in my hand. Trembling, I gripped it tight and pointed the barrel at Watts. "Stop right there," I warned.

He didn't stop, but lunged for my ankle. I danced away. "Stop! Now!"

He crawled forward on his elbows.

I aimed the gun at the ground near Watts's head and squeezed the trigger. The gun kicked so hard, I could feel the pain all the way up my arm. The gravel sprayed up in front of his face. He stopped.

Mom pushed up from the ground and limped over to where I stood, ears still ringing from the gunshot. She nudged Watts with her foot. "Valuable lesson, Damian. Don't mess with my daughter."

Ryan took control of the scene. It was weird to watch him in his agent's role. I preferred the image of laid-back college student.

While Mom held the gun on Stuart and Watts, Ryan grabbed some plastic zip-tie handcuffs from the SUV.

With Seth's help, he trussed them up like Sunday chickens and hauled them to the side of the road.

He asked me to retrieve his service revolver from where Stuart had tossed it. I brought it back to him gingerly. Despite what Stuart had said to cover for throwing the gun away, I was pretty sure it was loaded. I'd had enough of loaded guns for one night.

"Here you go," I said.

"Thanks, Aphra. I owe you one."

I shrugged and stepped back.

He snapped the gun into his shoulder holster. "I'm sorry about Seth's dad," he said.

"How did you—never mind. I don't want to know."

"That's probably best."

I looked at my hands. "I'm sorry we left you in the plane."

"It was a good call. You did what you had to do."

"It wasn't easy."

"None of it was. But you did good." He looked over to where Mom was talking with Seth. "Ever thought about following in your mom's footsteps and joining the Agency?"

"Not on your life."

He chuckled. "You know, I'm going to have to call for an ambulance."

"Okay."

"And because a weapon was discharged, there will be an investigation. I'll need to call for backup."

"Uh-huh . . . oh!" If he called for backup and Seth was still there . . .

He laid a gentle hand on my arm. "You know, Aphra, they can give me a ride, if you want to take off."

It took me a moment to understand his meaning. "So you don't need us to wait around until your . . . ride gets here?"

"No. I have things under control—thanks to you. Go on. Get going before I change my mind. Watts left the keys in the ignition."

"I don't understand. We can take the Escalade?"

"It's yours."

"You don't even want the ring?"

He shrugged. "Me, personally? No. It's not my style. The Agency? Well, I'm sure they'd like to look at it. But I think young Mulo over there needs it more than they do."

"You're letting us go."

"I'm giving you a head start."

I didn't know what to say. I gave him a quick hug. "Thank you, Ryan. I mean it."

"Hey, they told me to watch over you. Keep you safe. I'm just doing my job."

CHAPTER
13

We drove down the mountain in silence. In some areas, the mist was so thick that Mom had to slow the SUV to a crawl until we passed through it. She gripped the steering wheel during those times in a white-knuckled stranglehold. The glow from the dashboard lights illuminated her frown and the tenseness of her jaw. Time was running out. Every minute that passed was another minute Seth's dad was held captive.

About halfway down the mountain, an ambulance passed us going the other way, lights flashing, siren blaring. "They'll send the backup next," I murmured.

Mom glanced at me and then back at the road. "What?"

"Backup," I repeated. "He said he was going to call for an ambulance and backup."

She nodded, but didn't say anything for several miles. Finally, she spoke. "How long did you know?"

I furrowed my brows. "About?"

"Ryan. How did you know we could trust him?"

"I still don't know that we can. Maybe he handed off Stuart and Watts and he's on his way down the hill to get us right now."

She nodded. "He has a job to do." She stared straight

ahead, her mouth set in a grim line. "But I'm sorry you've had to learn not to trust."

"So am I." I closed my eyes and leaned my head against the seat back.

Ryan's words echoed in my head. *They told me to watch over you.*

There's a thin line between suspicion and paranoia and I hate to think I may have crossed it, but the more I thought about it, the more suspicious I became. The vehicle we were driving belonged to—and had been equipped by—the Agency. An Agency man had suggested we take it. Why?

It could be that he felt bad for the things that had happened. It could be that he was letting us go out of the goodness of his heart, but I didn't believe it. It was likely bugged. And there was no doubt in my mind that we were driving around in a huge tracking device.

Maybe Ryan sent us away—in his vehicle—because he wanted to see what we would say and where we would go. Maybe we weren't the endgame. Maybe we were pawns. Which meant we had to ditch the SUV. Fast.

My eyes flew open and I bolted upright. "I need to go," I said. "The first rest stop. It's an emergency."

Mom shot me a look. "Are you feeling all right? You want me to pull over now?" The concern in her voice almost made me want to cry.

"I'll be fine until the next rest area," I assured her. "But hurry."

We couldn't reach the rest stop quickly enough. I fidgeted more and more as each mile marker whizzed by. Mom kept giving me anxious glances and I'm sure she thought the worst.

"If you want me to pull over . . ."

"Rest stop, one mile," Seth called from the backseat.

Mom looked relieved. Not nearly as relieved as I was... or would be once we got rid of the Escalade.

The turn signal tapped a staccato rhythm as she pulled off the road and into the parking area. She switched off the engine.

"Why don't we all go," I suggested, "so we won't have to stop again."

Mom gave me a strange look, but thankfully she didn't argue. Seth, however, didn't seem to get the message. He made no move to open his door until I twisted around in my seat and gave him the evil eye.

When he got out I grabbed his arm and pulled him clear of the SUV. He followed, but hesitantly. I'm sure he thought I'd lost my mind. "What is going on?"

"It may be nothing." I glanced back at the Escalade. "It's just that back at the apartment Stuart said he tracked everything, like it was standard procedure. Then, of course, there was that tracker on the plane. And then when Ryan gave us the keys . . ."

Mom nodded grimly. "I wondered about that."

"So what are we going to *do*?" Seth asked.

I folded my arms. "We're going to get another ride."

• • •

Mom did the asking. We figured she'd seem more legitimate than a couple of teenagers, but still, I was amazed at how easy it was for her to swap cars.

She approached a guy who had stopped to buy a Coke from the vending machine. He was dressed in jeans and hiking boots, and wearing a North Face jacket. From where we were standing, I could see a large backpack in the back of his Jeep.

I couldn't hear exactly what Mom said, but it didn't take long for her to convince the hiker guy to trade vehicles with us. Even though it had been my idea, his response baffled me. I mean, he had to wonder why she would want to exchange a loaded, top-of-the-line Escalade—albeit with some bumper damage from the guardrail—for a rusted out, dented, plastic-for-windows Jeep. Normal people don't do things like that. Plus in our matching gray sweats and bare feet, we looked like escaped convicts or something. Wouldn't he at least consider that the Escalade might be stolen? But no, he didn't even balk.

"You're on," he said, pulling his Jeep key off of a jangling key ring.

"Where are you headed?" Mom asked—a little too casually, I thought.

"Up the pass."

"You going to hike the backcountry?" she asked.

He looked at her like she was an idiot. "Um, yeah." He stopped just short of adding, "Duh."

Perfect.

Mom and I stood together and watched him drive off. I hoped he enjoyed himself before the Agency caught up with him and demanded their property back.

We quickly inspected his Jeep. Mom was pleased to find that the gas tank was nearly full. That meant we wouldn't have to stop for gas for a long time. Which was a good thing, considering that we had no money. I found his registration paper in the glove box.

"He's from Bridgeport. Where's that?"

"About eighty miles from here. It's on the way to Spokane."

"We're going to Spokane?"

She bent to check the tire pressure. "I can access funds there."

The finality in her voice didn't invite questions, although I did wonder just how far-reaching that under-cover operation she had been working in was. I had thought it was just her, Joe, and Stuart, but she must have contacts elsewhere. How else was she going access anything without the benefit of identification? I real-ized anew that there was a lot about my mom's life that I didn't understand.

"You're sure he can reclaim his Jeep?" I asked her for the tenth time.

"We'll leave it in a tow-away zone. They'll impound it and send him notification."

With that, Mom climbed into the driver's seat and

fastened her seat belt. I hesitated. "Do you mind if I ride in the back with Seth?"

She glanced back to where Seth was settling onto the small backseat. I could read all sorts of caution in her eyes and I understood her reserve; she didn't want me to get hurt. But she and I both knew it was already too late for that. She sighed. "Fine. For now."

I climbed into the back and Seth pulled me close to him. We were together. That was all that mattered for the moment.

Mom turned the key in the ignition. After two tries the Jeep's engine roared to life. We rattled out of the rest stop—in the opposite direction from the Escalade.

Conversation was impossible inside the Jeep. The wind whistled through the flimsy windows and flapped the canvas roof. But I didn't really want to talk, anyway. The only thing Seth and I had left to say was good-bye and I wasn't ready for that yet.

We reached Bridgeport about one in the morning. It was a sleepy little town, snuggled up to the Columbia River. I knew that only because we had been driving alongside the river for several miles, and because a sign at the entrance to town proclaimed Bridgeport "Gateway to the Mighty Columbia River." The whole town was only about six blocks deep and maybe a couple dozen blocks long.

"Forget a tow-away zone," I said. "Everyone in town will probably recognize the guy's Jeep on sight."

"Yes," Mom agreed. "It does pose a problem."

"A problem? This makes it easier for him."

"For him, yes." Mom tapped her fingers on the steering wheel as we drove slowly down the street. "But it's going to make our borrowing another car unnoticed more of a challenge."

"Maybe we should keep going," Seth put in. "Ditch the Jeep in the next town over."

Mom shook her head. "Wouldn't do much good. There's nothing but small towns for at least another hour. Our hiking friend could have been picked up by now, and if so, we can't afford to stay with his vehicle even one moment longer."

We trawled the town along the waterfront until Mom saw what she was looking for. "Out-of-state plates," she said, pointing to a Toyota pickup that looked like it had seen better days. "It'll be snug for a while, but it will have to do."

I, of course, didn't mind being snug. I wasn't too crazy about the stale cigarette smell in the truck, but I was beyond being picky. We left Bridgeport—and the Jeep— behind and turned east toward Spokane.

Remembering my mom's advice, I snuggled close and rested my head on Seth's shoulder. We had a two-hour drive ahead of us, and after that, who knew when we could sleep? Wrapped in his arms, I closed my eyes and allowed myself to dream.

• • •

I woke to the glow of a Denny's sign. We were parked on the outer edge of the parking lot and Seth was shaking my shoulder. "Time to wake up."

Mom handed me a pair of cheap tennis shoes, the Wal-mart price tag still attached. "We're dumping the truck here. It's just a short walk to the hotel."

I tore off the tag and slipped the shoes onto my feet. I was too tired to question when she had bought them. *How* she had bought them. Had she already "accessed" her funds? In the morning I would look for answers, but for the time being, all I wanted to think about was a hot shower and a warm bed. And the fact that Seth would be with me a little while longer.

Seth and I waited on a bench in front of the hotel while my mom went inside to register. Neither of us said anything for a long while.

He picked up my hand, turned it over in his. I hadn't paid attention until then to exactly how filthy my hands were, with dirt caked black under my fingernails like a mechanic's. Blistered from bushwhacking. Unattractive. But Seth didn't seem to notice. He threaded his fingers through mine and looked into my eyes.

"I'll have to go soon," he said. "And then . . ."

I knew without hearing the words. Once Seth's dad was safe, the Mulos would move on. Seth would become someone else. He could not risk contacting me again.

"I wish it were different," he said.

"So do I." My throat was so tight, I could barely get the words out.

"Where . . ." His voice cracked. He cleared his throat and tried again. "Where will you go from here?"

I frowned. "I haven't really thought about it. I'm not sure if I can go home. Not until this is over." I didn't even know what "this" was, or if it would ever be over, but the words sounded right at the time.

"I'll think of you," he said.

I dropped my eyes so he wouldn't see the tears welling up in them. "I'll think of you, too," I whispered.

Mom came out of the lobby then, the tiredness etched deep in the lines of her face. I looked up at her, questioning. "Did you get a room?"

She didn't answer me. In fact, she didn't even look at me. "Seth," she said. "I need you to come with me for a moment."

Seth stood, and I jumped up beside him. I tightened my grip on his hand. I didn't like the sound of her voice. "Mom, what is it?"

She looked at me with sad eyes. "It will be easier this way."

I heard the car pull into the parking lot, heard it crunch over the gravel as it came nearer, but still I didn't want to believe it.

Seth pulled me close one last time. I clung to him, my tears soaking the shoulder of his sweatshirt, darkening the fabric. He stroked my back, my hair. His lips found mine and he kissed me deeply.

Behind him the car's engine idled. A man's voice said, "Seth. It's time."

Seth started to pull away, but I clung to him tighter.

He pulled my arms loose. "I have to go now," he whispered.

I wiped my eyes and tried to smile at him. "Say hi to your dad for me."

"Aphra—"

"No!" I stepped back. "Don't say it. I'm not ready for good-bye."

He brushed my lips with his one last time before he got into the car. And then he was gone.

Mom slipped her arm around my waist and stood with me. I laid my head on her shoulder. We didn't talk. We didn't have to. We watched the car drive away until its red taillights faded into the darkness.

epiLogue

My name is Marissa Vaterlaus and I'm about to begin the new semester at an exclusive boarding school in southern France. At least that's what it says on my visa.

According to the computer, I checked into a posh New York hotel three weeks ago for one last shopping fling before hitting the books. In actuality, I didn't become Marissa until today. This afternoon, in fact. I needed to remain Aphra Connolly long enough to send my dad a card. On the back I drew a picture of two forget-me-nots, intertwined. I hoped he'd understand.

It was a dangerous gamble, sending the message. The Mole seriously wanted Aphra dead and making contact of any sort gave him a location of origin to trace. But I couldn't let Aphra go without some kind of good-bye to her father.

Especially since she may never see him again.

I'll meet my mother in Paris tomorrow.
We have a lot of catching up to do.

Intrigued?

Read **Death by Denim**
to find out what happens next
to Aphra . . . and to Seth.